W9-AUA-072

DEMI'S FLUTE
ENTERING THE REALM OF SOUND

THE REALM OF SOUND SERIES: BOOK 1

By
Delandria Mills
&
Riley S. Brown

wunderlannd WP press

BALTIMORE, MARYLAND

1

Published by Wunderlannd Press
Wunderlannd Press Publishing LLC,
6 Dunhaven Place
Baltimore, Maryland 21236

Demi's Flute:
Entering the Realm of Sound
The Realm of Sound Series, Book 1

Front and Back Cover Art by Bryan Davis
Co-Illustrator/Design by Adam Jeremy Agee
Edited by: Doris Mills & Demetria Mills
Associate Editor: Tracey Romero
Permission to be used and copyright © 2015
Copyright Year: 2015
All rights reserved.

"When you play music, you discover a part of yourself you never knew existed."

-Bill Evans, American Jazz Pianist and Composer

For my loving parents, Doug Sr. & Doris, who always taught us to be ourselves and provided a home full of love and music.

For my siblings, Doug & Mimi who are the funniest, wittiest, and most loving brother and sister ever!

For EVERY music teacher who inspired me.

For every student of mine who inspired me through their wonder.

For Super Clyde the Wonder Dog, who was the sweetest dog a child could ever wish for.

Thank you all.

Love, Delandria

- Foreword -
By Delandria Mills

Demi's Flute stemmed from my desire to fuse the worlds of children's literature and music. My childhood was full of music. My siblings and I had a beautiful ongoing soundtrack playing throughout our young lives; from musicals my family watched together to the sounds coming from my father's portable battery-powered tape player as we played outside or helped our dad with lawn work. We would hear everything from Frederick Chopin to Count Basie to Brook Benton to Luciano Pavarotti.

I have the sweetest memories of: my Godmother snapping her beautifully-manicured fingers to the latest grooves while driving me around on weekends, my maternal grandmother washing dishes while humming along to Mahalia Jackson on the radio, and my cousin's boom box blasting away while many of the kids on my paternal grandmother's block were break dancing in her garage. When I was 4 years old, I remember the feeling I got while watching an uncle practice electric bass. I envisioned him having his own band, like the musicians I saw on television. More than anything, I really wanted him to have his own band.

I felt he deserved an audience. I was in awe of his ability yet had absolutely no idea what he was playing. I only knew that he seemed to be having fun and I could tell he felt it was beautiful. Therefore, I did too. I was not only moved by the marvel coming from his fingers, but the power it had to bring everyone together simply to watch and listen. For a few years, when I was six or seven years old, my mother enrolled us in summer reading programs at our local library. It was then that I fell in love with books.

Music, like words, has the ability to transport and inspire us all. I feel compelled to share how I began my musical journey as a child because it was fun and it has never stopped being fun for me. In recent years, the arts have taken a back seat to technology in the lives of our youth and in city schools. Demi's Flute encompasses the things I am most passionate about: music, education, and writing. I have a desire to see more children, as well as adults, expressing themselves through applied instrumental music. Demi's Flute is my contribution to that global cause.

-Delandria Mills
Author of Demi's Flute
December 29, 2014

DEMI'S FLUTE
ENTERING THE REALM OF SOUND

BOOK ONE
OF
THE REALM OF SOUND NOVELS

PROLOGUE

In a not-so-distant, seemingly altered future...

The café was an old one. It had been around for nearly a century, or that's what the young man had been told by the locals that lived around there. Martin Feldman snapped his brown satchel shut after putting his headphones and digital media player away and slid off his bike, chaining it to the nearest bike rack provided for the students that came from the campus nearby.

The cafe had changed in the last couple of years since the university had been expanded just a few miles away, that was for sure, Martin thought, looking around at all of the things that had been added.

No longer were there the old coin meters or

digital meters that printed out a ticket for you to put on your car's dashboard. Now, parking enforcement officers scanned the Aztec codes on each car's windshield. Even the old dumpsters were switched out. Fewer dumpsters and more community recycling bins were located on each block now, evidence of the ever-growing carbon-footprint-conscious generation that was slated to take over the quaint little town.

Martin stood in place and looked around for a few moments, taking note to see if the person he had come to interview had arrived yet. When he confirmed that he hadn't, the young college student moved for the entrance to the café and continued inside.

Upon entering, a cheerful bell alerted the Cozy Café staff of his arrival. Just inside the antechamber there was, as always, a small table, mirror, coatrack, and an umbrella stand waiting to greet as well. Martin took a quick glance in the mirror and, despite it being a dry day, he shuffled his shoes along the thick plush doormat out of habit.

The only new additions to this part of the

restaurant were the free publications spread across the little table and the "Community Happenings" corkboard. On the other side of the small room was the much larger dining area. Booths with wraparound seating spread out on either side of him in a fifties' diner fashion. Beyond that, two rows of tables and a bar with vintage swivel stools contributed to the motif. He took a seat at one of the tables in the center of the diner so he would be able to notice the person he was meeting once he came in.

*   *   *

"Would you like something before we begin?" Martin asked the old man once they were settled at the table. Martin was nervous, very nervous. He fiddled with his steno notebook several times and straightened the pens he had out on the table, looking to the old man for an answer.

The caramel-colored old man shriveled up his nose at the idea of food this early in the morning, but smiled nonetheless.

"I'll just have a coffee. Not much of a breakfast person." The young man waved the waitress over and ordered a pot of coffee, jotting down some notes on his notepad. The old man seemed somewhat intrigued.

"Taking down notes about what I eat, young man? I didn't know that was part of the interview."

Martin smiled. It was a young smile. The college student had barely broken into his twenties. He still had some small spots on his face from where acne had cleared up the previous summer.

"No, not exactly, Mr. Woods."

"You can call me, Devin. Most people I know do."

"Well, not exactly, Devin." He amended. "Much of what I write on this notepad are just things for me to ask you. I find things, from time to time, pop in my head and if I don't have this notepad, I will lose the thought and it will be gone forever."

The waitress brought over another clean, white cup and sat it down in front of the older man, pouring him a cup full of steaming, hot java.

"Thank you, dear." The waitress placed another few packages of dairy creamer in front of him and motioned to the sugar container at the far side of the table, where all the condiments sat together in a neat little pile.

"I have the same thing happen to me all the time. In fact, it's been so long since I've remembered something, I forget when I remembered it." The joke was somewhat dry to the young college student, but he laughed nonetheless, watching as the old man's face lit up, thick creases breaking over his brow and at the corners of his eyes. Devin took a small sip of the coffee after he fixed it the way he liked it, a light smile on his face as he sat the cup down.

"So, Mister-?"

"Feldman. You can call me Martin, or Marty, if you like. Feldman is so formal. I only remember being called that at the dentist's office or when I'm in line at the Department of Motor Vehicles."

"Alright, Marty. Marty," said the old man, reflecting to himself, "that's a good name. Marty. Strong name." He sat for a moment in silence and took another sip of coffee.

He seemed to sit with his thoughts a little bit longer. The old man contemplated things that weren't there, a past that Marty had yet to see, a world that had yet to be opened up before him as well as those in the coffee shop that were within earshot.

"What are you thinking about right now, Devin?"

The old man fiddled with his stirring spoon by the cup in front of him and looked around the café, trying his best to hide the smile on his face. But it came out anyway, and he didn't seem shy about it at all.

"So many things have changed since Demi..."

The young man scribbled in his notepad, this time it didn't seem to be about things he was going to ask, but more of thoughts that were moving between the two of them.

"I'm sorry. Did you say 'Demi'? As in d-e-m-i?"

"Yes, Demi. That was her nickname. That's what she was called throughout her youth."

"You said, 'changed since Demi.' What exactly does that mean?"

Old man Devin took another sip of his coffee, smiling that same smile that brought him to this conversation, this thought that he seemed so willing to share now with a complete stranger across the table from him.

"She changed things for a lot of people... a lot of people." He paused while Marty wrote down what he was saying. Devin leaned over and pushed the notepad down, flat on the table. He had something in his hand; a tape recorder.

"It's old but it still comes in handy sometimes." He handed it to Marty.

"Yes, quite handy." Marty dropped his notepad and fiddled with the buttons on the tape recorder. After pressing the record button, the small device started spinning the miniature tape inside around and around, recording everything around them.

"I figured your hand would get mighty tired writing all that I have to say after a while. Technology these days. Amazing, isn't it?" Marty nodded in agreement before realizing that the tape recorder was several decades old. He waved the thought away and continued with his interview.

"Where was I, again?" The old man fumbled for a hold on his story.

"'For all of us.' That was the last thing you said."

"Yes, for all of us. She helped to change so much, Demi did."

"I'm having trouble following you, sir. I mean, Devin. What, exactly, did she change and who is this 'us' you speak of?"

"I suppose I should start at the beginning, wouldn't you agree? I mean, bouncing around all over the place is not the best thing for me to do, now is it?" But the old man wasn't talking to Marty. Not at all. He seemed to be looking out somewhere far beyond the table, past the walls of the café, to some great beyond that only he could see.

Though Marty's recorder was on, he continued writing down tidbits here and there of what he thought was important. Devin's first line started like this:

"I guess it would have to be the moment that we first saw her alone up there."

*   *   *

Demi stepped out onto the dark brown mahogany stage. Her black, patent leather dress shoes broke the silence just after the applause had died down from the last student performers, 8th graders Jennifer McTeel and Susanna Morgan. They both stepped off the stage at the same time; one going off stage right while the other went left. Once seeing that the stage was clear, Mr. Tremelo prompted young Demi the rest of the way forward.

"Go on ahead, you'll do fine." It was more of a whisper from Mr. Tremelo. She couldn't see his lips moving when he said it. It wasn't his usual cheery voice from band class. There was something different, more serious, a tone she had yet to hear from him. His words didn't steady her or make her falter, but helped her realize that she wasn't alone.

Demi recovered, watching carefully as she placed one shiny foot in front of the other. Once she stepped from behind the crimson curtains, the sea of faces threatened to break the calm within her. She fought so desperately between the waves of excitement and anxiety.

Mr. Tremelo had told her what it would be like standing up in front of hundreds, the lights on her, the fear setting in, threatening to overtake her. Of course, the rehearsals and the performances with the band were completely different.

There, with the others, you could slip up, drop a note, or miss a riff, and you still had the safety of those around you to keep you focused in the moment.

But here, Demi thought, *here in the lights, onstage alone, is where I can get eaten up.*

Nevertheless, the flute is what steadied her, what kept her thoughts at bay, keeping her focused while refusing to let her buckle under the crushing weight of so many eyes.

This time tomorrow, it will be over. **If I make it** *through alive.*

She knew the tune well and had become very accustomed to appearing confident, despite the stage fright and the formal dress she wore.

In two hours time, this will all be over.

She put the flute to her lips, positioned her arms, elbows away from her body, and looked out into the audience, looking for familiar faces. And that's when she saw them -- her family.

There they were. They weren't difficult to find. DJ was attempting to sit tall enough to see Demi's shoes. Gayla was announcing in a very audible whisper, "There's Demi," while her parents, Jasper and Olivia, sat well dressed and smiling. They were all sitting in the third row, smiling up at her, waiting with loving, expectant faces.

That's when Demi began to change the world -- one melodic and glorious note after another. She did not waver. She did not look out again at the sea of faces but kept her stance, letting her eyes drift and drop from note to note. Turning the pages between notes, with each breath and each passing page, she played stronger and stronger until she allowed the music to do what it was created to do... consume her in its greatness.

-1-

"We all have ability.
The difference is how we use it."

– STEVIE WONDER

"Mom, do you *really* expect me to wear these?" Demi Woods' big brown eyes stared in disbelief at what her mother had done. Without fail, without even making it through the doors of her middle school for the first time, Demi's mother had wrecked her daughter's social life before it even started. Demi stared in disbelief at the three-button dress polo shirts, all five of them, and just looked at her mother in horror.

"This will end my life! My life's over! You have officially ruined my life, Mom!"

It wasn't an insult to her mother, of course. It

wasn't Demi's fault that her mother didn't know how to shop for her.

It was my own fault, Demi scolded herself. *I should have taken mom up on the offer of shopping instead of going to the movies with Deja.* The grave error of not taking the chance to shop for herself had suddenly fallen into the 11-year-old's lap. She knew that she would never do it again.

Red, pink, canary yellow, light blue, and neon purple. Those were the colors that her mother had picked out for her. It was like wearing a multi-colored target for ridicule.

"Demi, dear. We can always take them back."

Demi's mother saw the look of hurt on her daughter's face and tried her best to sell the soon-to-be 7th grader on the little felt teddy bears that dotted the shirts on the front and back. But Demi just shook her head. She knew she wouldn't take them back and couldn't bring herself to ask her mother to do so either. This had always been an unspoken rule of respect that she had for her parents; if they bought her anything, even if she didn't like it, she would accept it gratefully and carry on.

'There are starving people all over the world', 'You should be so lucky to have such good clothes'. 'Some people don't even have shoes on their feet or a roof over their head.' Demi heard these sayings from an assortment of adults throughout her short life and didn't feel like having them repeated any time soon.

No, she and her siblings, DJ and Gayla, were not ungrateful children. Under the tutelage of their parents Jasper and Olivia, the three children learned to appreciate everything that the world could offer them.

"Ruin your life? What are you talking about, baby girl? These are adorable!" Her mother ran her fingers across the little bears and smiled. "Your friends will love your little shirts."

Pressing her fingertips to her temples, Demi thought, *I can deal with this. It's just five shirts. It's not like the gift debacle from Christmas.*

The middle-schooler shivered at the thought of Grandma Johnson's itchy Christmas sweater with the light-up nativity scene on it as it came at her from inside the box, climbing stealthily out of the white tissue paper at its unsuspecting victim. And her parents made her wear it on at least three occasions before New Year's Eve, making her the laughing stock of her neighborhood.

But that was all in the past, Demi reminded herself, looking at the awfully juvenile polo shirts, knowing that they were more suited for early elementary school kids than her own middle school self.

No matter what, Demi knew that she would be okay, thanks to her strawberry-flavored lip-gloss. Her mother had done one thing right this summer; she bought a case of Demi's favorite lip-gloss, and now, much to the seventh-grader's pleasure, she had a lip-gloss applicator in every free pocket and even three 'back-ups' in the bottom of her backpack. If an apocalypse were to come, Demi would be well supplied and her lips would be as fresh as before the nuclear fall-out, smelling of a slight overdose of sweet, imitation strawberries.

And this is how the 1st day of middle school began for young Demetria Woods. She had seen a great many after-school specials on middle school and 'the child's transition into adulthood'. But it wasn't just the building, the other kids, or her adolescent mind getting the best of her. Middle school was known to be an awfully dreadful place that many could not imagine and a great many others still tried to forget.

Demi felt like she was on the frontlines. She had always felt this way ever since her two siblings were born. She was the first to lose her teeth, the first to go to school, the first to learn the truth about Santa and, much to her chagrin, the first to face middle school alone.

If she had a choice, she would have Clyde along for the ride. The old dog seemed to smile and frown up at her at the same time, watching as she got her backpack ready for her first day at a new school.

"I'd take you with me if I could. Yes, I would!" Her sweet-talking made Clyde's tail wag, just enough to pique her mother's interest in the morning routine.

"Don't touch that dog before you eat, Demi," said her mother. Demi fought the urge to scratch behind Clyde's ears and raised her outstretched fingers in a "surrender", stick-up fashion, slowly backing away from the dog. His tail was still wagging from the initial offer of leaving with her.

I'll go anywhere with you, Super Clyde's eyes seemed to say. But then again, they always seemed to say that.

Let's get out of here and ditch the grown-ups, play in a puddle, pee on a fire hydrant, bark at cats and curl up together on the floor and watch TV until we fall asleep. His eyes said all this and more, two of which he had talked Demi into doing over the years. Those doleful doggy eyes were very persuasive.

"Yes, mom. I'm not touching the adorable beast."

"Thank you. Now, please come in here and eat your breakfast."

"Coming."

I need to be quick, Demi thought to herself. It was 6:45a.m. The bus picks up at 7:15a.m. Her dad would be coming down the stairs in no time, paperwork and keys in hand, his eyes looking for the passenger he was tasked to speed away with in his car.

Demi put her book bag by the door and went into the kitchen for breakfast. Gayla and DJ were there too, with mom, getting their breakfast. Gayla waved to her big sister with a mouthful of Cheerios, some of them sticking out like crooked teeth.

"Hi, Demi," DJ squeaked, a half-eaten pancake on the end of his fork, dripping with maple syrup.

"Morning, DJ. Morning, Gayla." Demi kissed her little sister's forehead before sitting down next to her, looking at the spread that her mother had laid out for their first day of school.

There was cereal, bacon, pancakes, fresh fruit, eggs, and toast. Demi raked some fresh fruit from the bowl in front of her onto her plate.

"Fifteen minutes, Demi. Your dad will take you to your stop today, remember?"

"Yes, I remember." Demi chewed on a slice of cantaloupe while pouring herself a glass of milk.

This is how the morning went; nothing too grand. A comfy, quiet breakfast, and a quiet car ride with her father's playlist of music lightly coming through the speakers.

He always loved the old dirt road just outside the

house. He was so glad that the city hadn't paved over it and told Demi, time and time again, to look back with him to watch the dust swirl up behind the car as they drove away.

Each time Demi looked, there would be a different image swirling there in the dust, waving to them its goodbyes each day. Demi did her best to cover up the neon canary-yellow polo she wore, looking down at the little brown, felt teddy bears with a level of distaste she could not express with mere words.

By the time she had made the decision to finally accept the cheerful fuzzy bears, her father stopped just a few dozen feet or so from the bus stop where several kids were already standing. Most of them were 8th graders, standing there without their parents or family to watch them, but looking just as lost as Demi felt at the moment.

"Here you go, Demi gal."

"Okay."

Her dad leaned over and plopped a kiss on Demi's forehead, smiling to himself.

"You're going to do fine, Demi. I'm so proud of my

baby girl."

"Thanks, dad. But I haven't even done anything yet."

With a sigh and a soft smile, he said, "Yes, you did. You spent all of Christmas Break preparing for the audition to get into Templeton. And you got in! You did that, all on your own. Not many kids your age are that dedicated. I'll always be proud of you, Demi. Now run along before the bus comes. I'll be right here in the car until it leaves with you on it."

Demi's heart skipped a beat.

Right here? Why would you stay? I'm in middle school, now!

"Dad, it's okay. You don't have to wait. I know you have to get to work and everything."

"Don't you worry about me. Why wouldn't I see my baby girl off for her first day of middle school?"

Demi got out of the car and, with much reluctance, slowly walked her way to the bus stop, only looking back once. She knew what she'd find: her overexcited father waving out to her with a smile on his face. For some reason, Demi decided then and there at the bus stop, *it must be my parent's lot in life to embarrass me.*

When the bus finally pulled up, Demi was ready to get on it. Her father, however, caught her by surprise with a honk from his car, alerting all the kids getting on as well. Her father was waving to her as she tried to 'turtle it' and hide her head with her backpack.

Oh... my... God... so embarrassing.

Demi seemed to be waiting in line forever as the other kids loaded the bus ahead of her. She accidentally caught a glimpse of her father's smile and felt guilty for her level of shame.

I love you too, Dad.

-2-

"The way I feel about music is that there is no right and wrong. Only true and false."

- FIONA APPLE

Once the yellow school bus pulled away from her stop, the world somehow morphed into this somber, death sentence of a ride, as if not going to school at all. It wasn't like in the movies where dozens of kids were throwing things, talking, and goofing off with one another. It was early in the morning, the sun barely out, and all occupants on the bus completely quiet. None of the kids had the energy to do anything but sit silently in their seats and watch the world pass them by.

As Demi made her way down the aisle of seats, she

could barely see anything in front due to the darkness of the early morning. Even the lights on the ceiling of the bus weren't bright enough to light her way between the seats. To an 11-year-old, it looked like an endless pit of shadows. Demi couldn't see if anything was on the floor to trip over down there in the depths of the darkness, but she wasn't about to slip on the bus in front of all the other kids, especially on her first day. With a hand on each seat in front of her for balance, she conquered the darkness and moved ahead as the bus started down the road.

All around her, students looked longingly out of their windows, clearly upset in some way or another that summer had come to an end. School would now fill their free time with homework, projects, after-school activities, and rehearsals for a great number of events.

Demi felt that middle school was just one more step in the direction of becoming an adult. Something she couldn't begin to imagine.

It looked *so... SO... boring, yet busy and never ending.*

The bus ride wasn't so awful. After awhile, the bus finished picking up kids and was on the way to school.

There were five other buses dropping off behind Lawrence B. Templeton Middle School of the Fine Arts that morning when Demi's bus arrived. There was no way of knowing what to do or where to go once they exited the bus. It was as if, in this new world, instructions to students were no longer part of the equation. There was mass confusion and chaos when the new 7th grade students, Demi included, attempted to find their way into the school without guidance.

I'm not ready, Demi thought nervously as she trudged up the three steps to the main doors, carrying her lunch kit with her backpack over her shoulders, her flute case strapped across her body. Demi despised the idea that she was slowly becoming a grown up.

It was overwhelming to her. She hoped that she would be ready for adulthood when the time came but, for now, she was just hoping to get through the first day of middle school.

Alas, Demi eventually figured it out. For those who may not know, the first day at Templeton works like this: Students come into the building and are directed to a set of tables to receive their class schedules. They are then sent aimlessly wandering around a strange, new building, searching for their classes.

Once Demi got in line for the letters W though Z, she was at the table in no time, getting her schedule and locker assignment. After that, it was like being blindfolded and playing "pin the tail on the donkey". No matter which way she went, it was still difficult to find her first class.

The school was built like a huge square with various hallways emerging from every corner. The main four hallways of the square, if one could keep track, had classroom doors lining the walls. At each end and midway through, there were staircases with tall windows leading up to the second floor. The rooms that made up the inner square were for general studies and they overlooked a beautiful courtyard with benches, trees, and colorful flowers.

For the 7th graders, the bulk of their classes were on the west and south sides of the square on the first floor. So Demi made her way to the west side of the building to her 1st period class: Wind Band. She found the doorway marked 217 and walked in.

To Demi, the band room was spectacular. The ceiling was very tall and the back wall was made of cement and glass. The cement went from the bottom of the floor to about seven feet high with the rest of the almost 20-foot-wall made of glass windows. The windows exposed some of the lush trees outside near the playground and the sky. Demi knew at once that she would easily get lost in all kinds of daydreams looking out of those windows.

Upon walking into the room and passing the teacher's chair, she noticed that the floor was broken up like choral risers into five semi circles. After every three steps or so, students had to step up to the next level.

The first two levels were for the woodwind players, the brass section filled the third level, and the percussion instruments were set up on the two upper levels. On the left side of the room was an entire section dedicated to U.S. History facts complete with maps and pictures of historical figures on the wall.

Demi found herself catching the eye of President Roosevelt which she found odd and out of place in a music room.

The band room smelled like cork grease, rusty metal, and musty old music books. Although many would think that combination was gross, Demi loved the band room's smell. She had missed the smell of her elementary school's band room most of all. Harper Elementary's band room was a lot older and much smaller than Templeton's, so the aromas had less space to travel in.

Her band teacher looked like a crazy scientist with the exception that he didn't wear a lab coat. He did, however, wear a somewhat unusual mismatched sweater/vest combination. She would learn later as school progressed that he didn't care much for patterns and colors as separate entities. He would wear a polka-dotted vest with a striped shirt and solid tie. Other times, he would wear a checkered or argyle vest with a chevron-slated shirt and solid tie. No combination ever matched in the slightest.

"Good morning, class. My name is Mr. Tremelo and

I'm going to be your band instructor and homeroom teacher. For those of you beginning your first year here, I'd like to welcome you to Lawrence B. Templeton Middle School and I hope that it will go off without a hitch."

The middle-aged gentleman smiled at Demi and the rest of the class warmly, looking from face to face at those he had seen during the summer band auditions, as well as, the faces of those he had yet to meet.

In fact, Demi noticed, it seemed that Mr. Tremelo was trying his hardest to be as unfashionable as possible; Demi thought his outfit choices, as well as his disheveled hair atop his head, was a definite sign of that notion. And there, attached to his right hand, was a cup of coffee. Everyone, teachers and students, were aware of Mr. Tremelo's permanent fixture.

Whether he was walking the halls with a steaming cup in the morning or teaching a class in the afternoon with a stone cold cup'a'joe, Mr. Tremelo still drank from it. Demi wrinkled her nose at the idea of cold, day-old coffee. She knew even her dad wouldn't do that.

It was here in this class, that Demi also recognized a great many of her friends from her elementary school. Deja was one of her best friends who played the trombone. She was slightly taller than Demi, with long blond hair that reached down to the middle of her back. Many of the boys thought she was pretty, but Demi couldn't quite see why. Perhaps because she was always giggling and she had a cute but annoyingly high-pitched sneeze.

Then there was Oliver. He was a mild-mannered kid with an easy smile. He was slightly stocky with a complexion that looked very similar to rich chocolate -- she smiled as she remembered telling him so in kindergarten. His eyes did the same thing they always did and closed as he laughed. It was a trait he inherited from his mom, she recalled. Oliver had been Demi's neighbor before she moved into her new house. They graduated from Harper Elementary and enrolled in Templeton together. He smiled and waved when she had come in, pushing his thick glasses back onto his nose. His double bass rested next to him and he was finally almost as tall as it was. His trusty tuba was still in its case on the floor beside him. Demi waved back as she made her way to the first available seat she could find. She put both her lunch kit and flute case down on the floor beside her and took off her backpack so she could put all her school paperwork and her class schedule into it.

Then she noticed the boy from her new neighborhood, Josh, who played electric guitar. He was tall and thin and his complexion was that of a cappuccino. He had brown freckles scattered across his nose and cheeks and his hair was a tawny red, bushy Afro. He had let his Afro grow out during the summer and he was the closest thing to a hippie from Woodstock that Demi had ever seen in real life. He kept to himself and she rarely ever heard him speak. Even when he talked, he was so soft spoken that he could barely be heard. Upon noticing Demi, he nodded to her and gave her a half-smile, which was his usual.

Besides the 7th grade students Demi knew from her previous school, there was a slew of 8th graders in her class as well. She could tell by their height and their air of calmness and superiority at having survived the

7th grade unscathed.

Shane Thompson was one of these 8th graders. Demi remembered Shane well from elementary school. Shane and a small, select group of current 8th graders were hard to forget. He had been that awkward boy in the 6th grade that had grown faster and taller than anyone else. He was lanky, somewhat unsure of his steps, but even taller now. In a year's time, Demi noticed that Shane had grown into the once over-sized shoes and shirts that his older brothers had passed down to him.

The first thing Mr. Tremelo had Demi and the other students do was to stand up briefly to share what they did during the summer, what instrument each of them played, how long they'd been playing, and why they had chosen that instrument. For some reason, those forty-five seconds of sharing seemed like ten minutes of people staring straight at her.

As Demi left band, she noticed that Mr. Tremelo was on her schedule twice; once for Band Class, Session 1 and for 5th period's 7th grade Social Studies.

How can that be, Demi thought to herself, trying

her best to find her next class, weaving in and out of the rest of the crowd of lost 7th graders in the hallway, schedule in hand.

Demi's schedule looked something like this:

Period 1:	Band Class - Tremelo	217
Period 2:	Lang. Arts - Ellis	301
Period 3:	Art 1 - Pearl	Studio C
Lunch:	35 minutes	Commons
Period 4:	Gym - Mallory	Gym
Period 5:	Social Studies - Tremelo	217
Period 6:	Math - Geminny	209

It wasn't the end of the world, Demi thought to herself, finally finding her 2nd period class, all the way on the other end of the 7th grade hallway. Her schedule was airtight. One thing she did know was that the five-minute break between 1st and 2nd periods would be used just for getting to her classes.

At least I'm able to get a ten-minute break between Period 3 and Period 4. She noted that there was 35 minutes for lunch, 30 minutes to eat with an additional five minutes used for travel time. She only had one class she truly dreaded: Math. That was mostly because it was the last period of the day and would certainly sap what little energy Demi had left right out of her.

After trekking through the first few classes, finding a place to eat lunch in the crowded cafeteria, surviving the second half of her classes, enduring the bus ride home while being thoroughly exhausted, and from being more grown up than she had ever been in her young life, Demi was spent.

Her legs were tired and achy and she was famished beyond belief by the time she walked home from the bus stop. Her mother's smiling face was there to greet her when she got home though, which was a rare treat due to her mom's unusual workload.

"Hi, Mom!" Demi greeted quickly, then very happily turned towards the refrigerator. "Food!!!," she croaked as she shuffled, zombie-like, to the large shiny appliance.

From now on I'm eating breakfast in the mornings.

A full breakfast, Demi vowed to herself. "Don't bother," her mom called, "Come and sit at the table." Her mother could see the look of exhaustion on her daughter's face and slid a small plate of food in front of Demi.

"So," her mom inquired, eyes bright. "How many kids at school liked your shirt?"

-3-

"When you get to the end of your rope, tie a knot and hang on."

— FRANKLIN D. ROOSEVELT

The start of the second day was easy and simple. Demi woke up early, practiced her flute, and ate a *complete* breakfast, cleaning her plate this time. She was ready, attentive, and well fueled.

"Class, the ensemble auditions are posted. Be sure to look over who got the spaces that were available this year." That was the first thing Mr. Tremelo started with on the second day of school. During the first day of band class, Mr. Tremelo prepped the students well. He gave them a thorough overview of his expectations so the students would be ready to hit the ground running by Day Two.

Before the late bell rang, none of the band students had a chance to look at the audition results posted on the door of Mr. Tremelo's office. So, of course, it taxed everyone to the point of near lunacy waiting to see how they were going to be placed for the year. Right away, all of the students were sent to practice rooms in groups, referred to as Sectionals. Each practice room had a digital tablet at the door with a playlist of the pieces each section was required to listen to after sight-reading each new piece of music.

Demi had trouble focusing during the flute sectional. An undergraduate student from a nearby college was conducting all of the flute students that day. Aileen was a lanky, twenty-something sporting a short, pink Mohawk. After spotting Aileen's purple fanny pack and the water bottle on the young woman's hip that read *Life Cycles*, Demi guessed the young intern had ridden her bike to Templeton.

Mr. Tremelo directing us to work together on pieces of music without knowing how we rank amongst each other is slightly uncomfortable.

Demi thought the half-hour flute sectional was sheer torture and wondered if anyone else felt the same way. After practice, she discovered that most of the others did, too. Even from the brass section, she had it confirmed by the awkward smile of Shane, who sat himself in the 3rd chair trumpet seat.

First period was about to end and the students were told to put away their music, help align chairs, and to place the music stands on one of the racks found on the right side of the room. Demi got in line to put away her music stand. Somehow she joined into a conversation with the five trumpet students.

"Yeah, he did this last year, right Ethan?" Shane's friend and other band mate nodded his closely-shaven head in agreement.

"Yeah, last year Tremelo had new ways of torturing us regularly."

"But why?" Demi asked.

Shane piped up in response.

"I'm sure he thinks he's preparing us for life as a musician. You know, working together despite the pressure. Maybe it's to make us take ourselves less seriously." He paused. "But I'm sure he wants us to learn something from it."

Demi could tell that Shane had a lot of respect for Mr. Tremelo, but she also knew that selecting chairs wasn't a game for her.

At her elementary school, there were fourteen flute students and she worked her way up to second chair by the end of her fifth grade year and first chair by the end of sixth grade. She had known all too well back in elementary school that the flute, for her, was not to be taken lightly. Her old band teacher, Mr. Wayne, was committed to assist even the youngest student to become a virtuoso if he or she desired to be one.

Mr. Tremelo's summer auditions were pretty straightforward. Students were given the following to prepare: a list of major scales to play, an etude to prepare, excerpts from the band music they were going to be playing in the fall, as well as a suggested listening guide. Included in the packet was an audition appointment schedule, which was to take place one month later.

Next in the audition process, Mr. Tremelo and a few of his interns would deliberate over how well the incoming students played and selected chairs for the band accordingly.

At least that's the way it was supposed to go. Students who auditioned in the summer were to be placed in band based upon their auditions. Practice sheets were also considered in the process because they gave Mr. Tremelo an idea of how hard a student was willing to work.

After placing her music stand on the rack, Demi decided to wait until the rush of kids were gone from the roster to look at it. With a few minutes left before the late bell for her 2nd period class, Demi looked on the roster and searched for her name, knowing that she had prepared as best she could. After all, she spent most of her vacation practicing or participating in summer music camps.

Demi knew that acquiring the first flute chair in Templeton's band was not for the faint of heart. Only those who were willing to put in the work dared to be a section leader. The first chair of every section was a difficult seat to hold and one did not go very long without being challenged by other members for the first chair.

Sure, those who were "born virtuosos" accomplished the task of landing the first chair with very little effort. And, of course, most of the band was simply at Templeton because it was known as the "go-to" school if you wanted a chance of getting into a Fine Arts high school. For Demi, this was her first defining moment at Templeton.

Then she saw her chair placement. Not exactly where she had expected it to be. Apparently, 1st chair in elementary school meant very little in middle school.

Ninth chair? It was all Demi could do to restrain herself from tearing the post down, ripping up the paper with her name and everyone else's into little, tiny, itsy-bitsy pieces.

Suddenly, all of Demi's summer came flooding back into her mind, like one great tidal wave, clearing all of her good thoughts away completely.

Her hopes of getting one of the first flute chairs, which usually consisted of one of the first four or five chairs, and perhaps the chance to perform during the spring concert, now grew dim in her eyes.

Next to the roster were sheets with a student's name, grades, and assigned band chair that said: **'Waiver. Parent signature required'.**

I don't want my parents to see this. After countless hours of practicing, listening, taking notes, and watching videos, I placed ninth? For some, chair assignments mean very little. Heck, most of the students are just happy to be at Templeton.

Demi sighed heavily.

While the rest of the kids in my neighborhood were outside playing, going to the movies, staying up late at summer camps that had them swimming, boating, and telling stories by the campfire, I was sitting in my room, day after day, practicing... Ninth chair?

Demi's face was flushed. She felt like crying. Then she thought about Mr. Tremelo.

It's no big deal. He just doesn't know me. Maybe I should ask Mr. Wayne to talk to Mr. Tremelo. Maybe this has been posted as some type of challenge. I officially hate Templeton. If this is what the Templeton band experience is going to be like, perhaps I'll give up now. Seriously, I may get more accomplished just playing along to dad's recordings of Solti conducting at home.

Demi rushed away from the list on the wall, bee lining it to her locker, almost forgetting that she had a second period class. She put her flute case down next to her locker and spun her combination in the lock. She pulled. It didn't budge. She tried it again.

18-right, 22-left, 9-right. I know that's my combination! Why isn't it working?

She pulled again... and again. Nothing. It wouldn't budge at all. Everything was working against her today. She could feel the tears welling up in her eyes.

Ninth chair! You've got to be kidding me!

Demi let her books drop to the floor. She imagined looking around for the balloons, the cameras, and the crazy t.v. show host who would pop out at any minute and say that this was just some new reality show and she was Punk'd or something to that effect. But no one showed. Well, no one she expected, that is.

But Shane was there and had been standing behind her the whole time, apparently waiting for her to finish so he could get to his locker next to hers.

He smiled at her, that weird, awkward, "I really didn't need to see all of that" smile. If Demi could be anymore flushed, now would be the time. She attempted to fumble with the lock, but then looked down at the books and flute case on the floor. She couldn't pretend with Shane. He had seen her get upset and she hadn't even noticed him the entire time.

"You need help with your locker, Demi?"

"I...um.. don't... know-"

Apparently I've lost the ability to speak or form words as well, Demi concluded. She did her best to regain her composure as Shane came closer, books in his hands.

"I'm at 405. Yours is 409, right?"

Demi nodded her head, turning away for a brief second to wipe away the tears that had formed at the corners of her eyes. She sniffled once and contained herself.

Demi put on a fake smile from ear to ear, trying to remember to breathe, smile, maintain control, and all the other things a girl has to remember when looking into her crush's eyes. But there was too much going on inside of her head to care at the moment.

"Four-o-nine was mine last year. It's a bit tricky, but once you know how to use it, you get the hang of it."

He put his trumpet case down and, without a hitch, spun the combination lock around a few times and opened it for her.

"I'm sure you'll get the hang of it. Just give it some time."

In the midst of all this madness, Demi had noticed something; everything Shane did was somewhat awkward to the rest of the world, but Demi just ate it up. In the brief time she had known Shane in elementary school, she had always known him to be a good kid.

After he helped her, she thought she was free and clear of Shane, picking up her books, but he stayed and helped, lingering a little longer before opening his own locker.

"Are you okay, Demi? I noticed you running away pretty fast from class a minute ago and I just wanted to—"

"I'm fine, Shane. Thanks."

What a great lie I just told, Demi thought to herself.

"You know, if it's about the chair list, I wouldn't worry so much. Tremelo has a way of making changes and choices along the way, you know, throughout the year."

Demi just nodded in understanding, knowing she tended to take herself too seriously at times.

It just hurts to see myself so far down from what I expected, that's all, Demi thought.

When Demi's dejected face didn't change, Shane finished getting his things from his locker and closed it, saying, "Well, from what I heard, you weren't half bad. But that's just coming from me."

But, coming from Shane, it did make a difference. Demi managed a half smile.

"Thanks, Shane."

He smiled back.

"No problem. Well, gotta go. Gonna be late to Ms. Patterson's class if I don't leave now. Later, Demi."

"Later." Demi's goodbye caught in her throat and died out before it could make it to Shane's ears. And then he was gone.

I wasn't half bad? What Mr. Tremelo's list had torn asunder, Shane's compliment began to build up again.

The rest of the day came and went like the first day, with the exception of actually getting homework from all of her classes.

Even gym class gave me homework, Demi exclaimed to her inner self, eyeing all of the parental paperwork that she had to get signed and bring back by the end of the week.

Gym uniform requirements, medical release forms, gym code of conduct and ethics, photo release form and, finally, the gym physical form and appointment date. Whew!

Demi had never needed a physical before because she had never played any sports, with the exception of the occasional kickball during recess and various sports during Field Day at the end of the year at her elementary school.

Now, apparently, you need as much paperwork as the Olympics just to be in a middle school gym class!

Both Mom and Dad had always looked at her stuff from school. However, it was different this time. Her father looked at the school's take-home materials and her mother looked at the work done in each of Demi's classes. That's what they had agreed to before she started middle school. They had both been able to work on the elementary school things together, but now that Demi was moving up in the ranks of her schooling, her mother and father divvied up the work between them, especially since they had DJ in third grade and Gayla going to pre-K this year.

She thought her parents were pretty amazing. They gave so much of themselves and still had time to be brilliant individuals. Once, Demi's dad helped her with a school project, spending all of a Friday afternoon and an entire weekend on it with her even though he had work to do himself, which he completed after Demi had fallen asleep, staying up late into the night, far past his own bedtime.

When the final bell rang for release, Demi was happy to get on the bus. With Mr. Tremelo's posted results far from view, she was ready to just let the bus take her away and zone out until she got home, where she could sit with Super Clyde and have a chance to regroup.

As she boarded the bus, she noticed there were more students than there had been before, barely leaving any seats available. The morning crowd that she had expected of twenty to twenty-five students had now doubled to nearly forty faces, most of them she didn't recognize at all.

They must have gotten rides to school on the first day, Demi thought.

She looked for a seat that she could have all to herself, but there was no chance of that, so she would have to sit with someone. The thought of socializing, after the day she'd just had, did not sound appealing at all. As the bus doors closed behind her, she knew she'd better take a seat and quick. There were still a few other kids in the aisle looking for seats, as well.

"You can sit here." A voice piped up just a few seats in front of her, nearly halfway down the bus. The owner of the voice wore long, light brown braids and a welcoming smile. She seemed a little more mature than Demi due to her modelesque features accentuated by the perfect application of her make-up, although she too was a 7th grader. Demi nodded thanks and plopped down next to the girl, adjusting her backpack, lunch kit, and flute case so they'd all fit in her lap.

"Thanks."

"No problem. I'm Cora Angelica Jones. My family calls me Angel, but most of my friends call me Angelica."

"Demetria Mikayla Woods. Everyone calls me Demi." Announcing her full name felt odd, but she only did so since it was how Angelica introduced herself.

What happened then was pretty cool.

They began to talk and, sooner than expected, Demi

had made a new friend. Demi laughed at Angelica's endless jokes and together they laughed about the kids that popped up when the school bus hit potholes along the way. Angelica asked hundreds of questions. Being a bit shy, Demi really appreciated Angelica's interest and ability to keep the conversation so lively. After what felt like question number three hundred and eighty-six, Angelica asked about the case Demi was carrying.

"It's my flute. I've been playing it since fourth grade. I'm in Wind Band and, in my spare time I write songs."

Their conversation lasted until Angelica got off at her stop, which was only four stops before Demi's. Demi grabbed her things and got up, letting Angelica get out of the seat. They waved bye to one another and Demi felt better.

Maybe ninth chair is not the end of the world after all, Demi thought to herself.

She got off at her stop and took the sunny afternoon walk with the thoughts of her future in middle school floating in her head. Her thoughts were of Shane and his smile, his comforting words, the possibility of moving up in chairs before the end of the semester, and having a new friend in Angelica.

Throughout the entire summer, Demi hadn't spent any time with her old friends. Actually, she didn't have many friends. The only time she had a sizable group of friends was when she lived in her old neighborhood near Oliver and Deja. They and many of her other friends went to their first summer band camp together, just before Demi moved.

Demi made a decision then. She would start to have a life. Now that she was in middle school and growing up, she would make some friends and hang out more. It was time to be more than just 'the flute girl' who practiced all the time.

When she got home, she had a thousand things to tell Clyde. It had been some time since she and Clyde had talked, so sitting down for a 'confession session' would be easy this time.

She waved to her father, who was in the kitchen.

"Hey, big girl. Dinner will be late tonight. There are some snacks laid out for you kiddos on the table."

Her father smiled at her. Demi placed her backpack and lunch kit on the kitchen counter, noticing her siblings fast asleep stretched out on the couch in front of the TV with their usual after school cartoons playing. She then proceeded up the stairs towards her bedroom with her flute case and band folder.

"Okay. Thanks, Dad." She made her words just loud enough so her father could hear them as she continued to her room.

"Clyde, you are not going to believe the kind of day I've had. It all started with me getting ninth chair. Ninth chair, can you believe it?! Then—" Demi stopped herself, looking down at Clyde.

He didn't move or jump up like he usually did when she came into the room. In fact, he didn't even lift his cute little face or wag his tail. As she came nearer, he finally lifted his head, his tail wagging listlessly. She rubbed his head and sat down next to him.

"What is it, boy? Not feeling so super today?" She felt his nose; it was warm and dry. Super Clyde wasn't doing so well.

"Dad. Come here, please!"

"What is it, Demi?" But upon entering the room, her father could see Clyde for himself. They both knew something was very wrong.

-4-

**"People compose for many reasons;
to become immortal; because they have
looked into a pair of beautiful eyes; for no
reason whatsoever."**

- ROBERT SCHUMANN

It was—
Kidney failure.

Clyde loved to pee on things, Demi reminded
herself. *Fire hydrants, bushes, stranger's legs, and her
mother's rosebushes that never seemed to grow so
wonderfully until they were visited upon by Super
Clyde the Wonder Dog in the early spring every year.*

*   *   *

Demi's mom and dad picked their kids up from school the next day and, together, they took Clyde to the veterinarian. It didn't take the doctor long to make his diagnosis. After a blood test and a few other tests, (Demi didn't really comprehend it all), the doctor told them that it was simply age kicking in.

"It was bound to happen at some time or another. Clyde—"

"Super Clyde," Demi corrected quietly, holding her poor dog's paw while he lay on the vet's cold, metal table.

"Well, ah, Super Clyde," amended the vet, "is at that age where his health is starting to wane. He's getting older. It's a natural process, really." But to Demi, that wasn't good enough. There had to be something more that they could do for Clyde.

We can't just let him die. He's not even that old! Grandpa's dog, Leitrim, saw my aunt Lorraine through high school and well into her marriage.

The vet suggested medication and gave it to her parents for Clyde to take in order to retain water and flush his kidneys out. It was more of a natural remedy solution than a sedated state of mind until he lost himself altogether and slipped away.

Demi wasn't new to the death of a beloved pet. Years ago, when she was just a little girl and DJ had just been born, she remembered having a pet rabbit that had gotten sick. It came down with a sickness that it never recovered from, no matter how much love Demi and her parents gave it. The rabbit passed away and Demi remembered watching, with a heavy heart, as her father carted it away in a blanket. She knew DJ and Gayla, along with herself, would be devastated to lose Clyde so soon.

I'm not having that for Clyde! I don't want him to be "carted" away, never to be seen again. It's too soon and that's that. I won't let that happen without a fight.

Based upon what the veterinarian said, there was nothing the family could do except provide medication for Clyde that would prolong his life and keep him out of pain until the end came.

The doggy doctor apologized several times, patting Demi on the shoulder, trying his best to assure her parents that medication was the best solution.

The family had been there for each other through thick and thin. Even the pets got the love they deserved when they became part of the Woods family. The only thing Demi could do was bear the news and go on as best she could. At least, that's what the look in her parents' eyes said to her when she tried to smile through her tears.

The night didn't go so well after that. It was rough for Demi and the rest of the family to sleep, especially since they knew that Clyde would need attention.

Instead of him sleeping in Demi's room like he normally did, her parents put him between the kitchen and the dining room downstairs, laying out a small doggie bed for him to sleep in. It was the one used by Clyde until the day he decided he would no longer sleep alone, claiming part of Demi's bed as his own.

What help can I give other than just being there for him? What would he do if I were sick?

Of course, Demi knew exactly what Clyde would do if she weren't feeling well. She had experienced Clyde coming to her aid several times in her younger years.

He had always been the hero at her bedside whenever she needed him; lovingly licking her face as if he were trying to reduce her fevers, waking her up in the middle of the night while trying to get comfortable at her feet when he was supposed to be letting her rest after she'd fallen off her bike and sprained her ankle, as well as singing to Demi his sweetest lullabies on a few of her sleepless nights, annoying a handful of neighbors in the process.

That's what I'll do! I'll write a song for Super Clyde, affirming his wellness.

Some of Demi's best ideas came when all was quiet and the rest of family was asleep. She felt this was when her favorite melodies were written.

Composing a song for Clyde would at least keep my mind off of his sickness and on the good times I've shared with him.

She laid out a handful of blank sheet music and grabbed a couple of sharpened pencils from her nightstand. There, on her island away from everyone and everything, she sat over her blank staff paper and began to write.

The song began first as a single note, the lead of her pencil tracing the single note, over and over again, nearly breaking through the surface of the paper, until the next note came out through the fog in her head.

*Clyde is doing **just fine**,* she further convinced herself so as not to get caught up in the negativity of what she had heard at the vet's office.

What would he like to hear that would make him feel even better?

Demi looked at the flute case in front of her on the bed, her free hand reaching out to it, unlocking the clasps that held it closed. In moments, she had pieced it together and had it in her lap as well, testing the notes she had written down.

And that was when the world around her began to drift away like an unmoored boat at the docks, slowly slipping out of view as the notes became more prominent in Demi's mind.

More Super... More Wonder... Less Clyde, she thought to herself. She erased one note, and then added another in its place. *The Clyde part comes at the end of the song,* she told herself, placing a few more notes on the bar, testing the combination of them with her flute, letting the melody come to her without force.

There she was, on the island, far away from everyone; far away from the problems of her world, of the traffic and the noise of the city not so far away, far from the sad look on Clyde's face when she passed him downstairs as she went to bed earlier.

What she saw, and what made the notes on the page in front of her, was the old Clyde, the Clyde she had known throughout most of her life. The first few notes were reminiscent of the way Clyde made her feel when she was around him, of what the "Super" meant in his name and how it spoke to the world and made strangers laugh upon introduction in the dog park.

In time, the notes on the page progressed into an array of passages that personified Clyde. Light and melodic at first, similar to the first few steps a not-so-sure footed Clyde had taken as a puppy when Demi first saw him. Soon, the puppy grew into a short-lived menace that chewed up everything he could get his mouth on, with small blasts of shouts and barks of protest from the family, also turning into notes. Small sections reserved for the feelings that Clyde had when being scolded began to appear on the pages as well.

Soon, the scolded Clyde in the corner had become a block of notes, repeated over and over again until it was almost comedic, slapstick, even.

Demi could faintly hear movement downstairs even though her door was shut tight. Her island was undisturbed by her brother, sister, or parents.

Clyde wouldn't want me moping about. He would want me to be having fun and playing and living my life. At least, that's what I think Clyde would want for me. That's what I'd want for him if I were sick.

Just then, she pictured herself sick in bed, coughing and sputtering sentence fragments, petting her dog on the head and telling him to go play outside.

And Demi saw it -- the young puppy that had always come out in Super Clyde's eyes had him jumping and rolling through piles of leaves in the fall, chasing the ice flurries in the winter, even jumping in a few streams and ponds to fetch a floating stick that had been thrown out into the bayou nearby.

Grabbing the first few pages of the song for Clyde and her flute, Demi slipped her house shoes on and glided past her brother and sister's bedrooms as well as her parent's, making her way downstairs to her best friend in the whole wide world. She bypassed the creaky spots on the stairs rather easily and walked into the room where Clyde's doggy bed was sitting.

The only light on was the small bulb over the stove, some of it shining into the dining room from the kitchen. Demi sat in what light she could and laid the sheet music in front of her on the floor, covering her crossed legs with her night gown as she got comfortable next to her sleeping Super Clyde.

He looks rested but tired, Demi decided, not wanting to wake him for anything but an emergency.

If the doctor insisted on giving us the 'this is the beginning of the end' talk, I guess I should do this now.

But the old pup didn't hear her thoughts or her movements beside him. His ears and eyes were still at the moment and his breathing had become a bit labored.

"I wrote this for you, Clyde. It's not finished, but

it's what I've got so far."

Demi straightened her back and began to play. It was the Super part of the song first. The melodic notes crept in through the darkness and broke the silence in the room. Demi barely whispered the notes into the flute, her hands moving more quietly than they had ever moved before, her fingers gracing the keys on the flute, letting the song play itself out.

There was a single twitch from one of Clyde's ears, his left ear, and that was enough for her.

-5-

"Art is a subject inundated with opinions. In fact, that's all it is about is opinions."

- CHICK COREA

The most miserable and the happiest moments of Demi's middle school life somehow plotted against her and prepared her for a sabotage sandwich.

How is it possible to have two feelings that are such opposites at the same time?

That morning, she had gotten up with only one thing on her mind. It wasn't which chair she got in band, whether Shane liked her, or if she truly had a new friend in Angelica. It was Clyde.

But it wasn't just her little world around her that seemed to be harboring negativity and sadness; the weather was, too.

Demi sloshed along the path to the bus stop. She

remembered just worrying about whether or not her dog was able to go potty correctly and be able to keep up with her antics when he was just a puppy. At this thought, Demi's eyes began to water, her sadness nearly making her burst at the seams. And her seams weren't stitched very strongly at the moment.

Following the path to the bus stop, clad in her galoshes, Demi tried her best not to let the thoughts of her ailing pup affect her. It had rained a lot recently in Southeastern Texas, more than usual, but *today was no joke.*

Even the gargantuan puddles were not something you wanted to jump in!

Ahead of her, there were a multitude of brown and dark brown mud puddles waiting for any unsuspecting victim, blocking all safe passages to the bus stop. She took measured steps so as not to step into any of the muddy, lake-sized booby-traps. She had done that before a time or two and the muddy water had found its way up past the edge of her rain boots.

She had tried her best to get the mud stains out of her socks, but it was useless. Even with her mother's "magic" formula for the wash, the mud stains still remained today.

Today though, Demi managed to make it through the minefield unscathed. The morning bus ride was uneventful. When Angelica sat with her she seemed somber but Demi thought it might have been due to the woes of early morning. The conversation was light and Demi told Angelica about Clyde while Angelica told Demi about her crazy homework from the night before.

The entire school population was either wearing galoshes and a raincoat or toting an umbrella, with much of the hallway looking as though it were going to break into a musical number, twirling wet umbrellas to music in unison. Although none of that happened, Demi snickered at the idea.

Band rehearsal went well that morning. Demi was pleased with the flute section. However, it was a few classes later when things began to get interesting for her.

Fifteen minutes before the first bell rang, while in the library, Demi lifted her math book in front of her, watching Shane as he made his way across the courtyard and into the library. He slid his book bag from his shoulder and onto the floor in one fluid movement as he sat just two tables in front of Demi with his buddy Ethan. He slid ever so neatly into the chair.

"I'm soooo tired!" Shane declared as he pulled his homework out.

"Dude, where were you last night? I waited up until ten! I thought we were gonna waste'em online!" Ethan looked a bit flustered when he said this.

Demi got her math homework and notes out, knowing quite well she'd need to stay focused to keep up in Mrs. Geminny's class. She continued to listen intently behind her book, all the while pretending not to be interested at all.

"Sorry, man! I had to practice last night. If I'm gonna get a spot in the recital, I'll need to up my game a little bit."

"Yeah, I know what you mean. Did you hear that new girl yesterday?"

New girl, Demi thought. *Is he talking about me?*

"Yeah, she really killed that flute solo!"

Flute solo? I was the only one yesterday that... *They **are** talking about me! Oh my god! Shane is actually having a conversation about* **ME!**

Demi nearly toppled her book onto the floor in response to hearing them.

Did I really leave that much of an impression on them, Demi thought. Demi had never believed that she had left any kind of impression on anyone in her life. So, the fact that someone had taken a notice of her, and her playing no less, was worth contemplating over.

So that's just what Demi did; she thought about what kind of impact she made on everyone; from her teachers at her old school to her family and then to her friends at school. Little did she know, she would soon get a response to that thought quicker than she expected.

Demi had never known what a bully was firsthand. Not in her years at Harper, in Girl Scouts, or summer camp had she ever encountered anyone who didn't want to be friends with her. She had always had an easy way of falling into a group of kids and making friends quickly, although she didn't mind her own company.

So, it was quite a surprise when her friend Angelica Jones decided to become just that. Demi had just gotten onto the bus for the afternoon ride home when she noticed Angelica sitting with someone else. She threw a quick smile and wave to Angelica before taking a seat.

"Hey, Demi! Gonna play that flute for us today, huh?"

The question was harmless but the intent behind it and its sarcasm was so thick that Demi could cut it with a knife. Demi just chose to ignore it and take a seat somewhere else. She was on a happiness high, still thinking about Shane and the comments he had made. She put her ear buds in and began listening to the piece she was interested in playing for the recital.

Apparently, Angelica wanted some kind of attention though. Angelica moved to another seat on the bus, this time sitting directly behind Demi. Angelica pressed her knees into the back of Demi's seat, pushing her forward a bit. This time, other students on the bus took notice of what Angelica was trying to do, their eyes going to Demi to see what her response was going to be.

Demi's sudden friend-turned-foe piped up again, this time louder.

"What is it, Diiiii-meeee? Cat got your tongue? Or should I say Wonder Dog? What's wrong? I heard your doggie's not feeling so well these days. He getting worse or something?"

Demi could feel her blood boil. Her face became warm and she bit her lower lip to keep the distaste from seeping out of her mouth and giving in to Angelica's taunts.

I confided in her about that! I didn't expect her to go blabbing about it to everyone on the bus.

But Demi didn't want to seem weak, so she answered back in the best way she knew how.

"Leave me alone."

Demi could tell that it took a few moments for Angelica to think of a comeback for this. She was silent behind Demi for almost a minute before she started back up again.

"So yeah, I'm bothering you now? Is that what it is?"

"What's going on with you, Angelica?"

"What? Like, do I have a problem with you?"

"Yeah."

"Well, I do. What are you going to do about it?"

Demi noticed Angelica passed her stop a while ago and assumed she must be staying at a new friend's house. And that's when Demi's stop approached and the bus came to a halt.

"Oh, saved by your stop. We'll continue another time, flute girl! Don't think this is over!"

Demi didn't think anything of the sort. In another few moments, she was away from Angelica and her taunting. Demi watched as the bus doors closed and continued down the road onto the last few stops without her. Demi looked down the dirt road to her house that was a little less than a mile away. She couldn't wait to get there and figure all of this out.

What was that all about, Demi thought to herself.

But the middle-schooler didn't have time to think about what had just happened on the bus. Once she arrived home, all she could think about was Clyde.

It was her mother who was there when Demi arrived at home.

"Hi, baby girl!"

"Hi, Mom. How is Clyde doing?"

"He seems to be doing okay. Each of us will need to watch his progress. His spot down here makes taking him out a little easier. Some of the medication is making him feel out of sorts, so we need to make sure that he eats when he's supposed to and gets his medicine at the right times. I think you should take the first watch today. I'm sure he will be happy to see you, especially since you've been spending so much time practicing upstairs these days."

Little did Mom know I came downstairs and played for Clyde last night, Demi reminded herself, not feeling so guilty for keeping herself busy during his time of illness.

"Okay, mom. That's fine."

Her mother showed Demi where Clyde's medicine was, how to give it to him, as well as the dosage amount to give. It was fairly easy. Clyde didn't really put up a fight when it came time to take his medicine. He just went with it.

Her best friend looked up at her with sick, sad eyes when she approached.

"How's my Clyde of Superness doing today, huh?" He leaned into Demi's hand as she rubbed behind his ears, his eyes closing comfortably.

And weakly, Demi noticed, her friend of so many years laid his head in her lap once she sat down beside him.

"I'm here for you, boy." His eyes looked up as if to say, *Tell me about your day, Demi.*

Demi obliged and began...

"You'll never believe what happened to me today."

And, like a tried and true best friend, Super Clyde listened attentively to everything Demi had to say, without interrupting her once.

-6-

"I've always known I was gifted, which is not the easiest thing in the world for a person to know, because you're not responsible for your gift, only what you do with it."

- HAZEL SCOTT

Though Demi didn't get a chance to talk to her parents about the bully on the bus, she did manage to slip in a last-minute conversation with her dad before he left, asking if he could take her to school today.

"Sure thing, hon'. What do you need the lift for?" Her dad wasn't being nosy; he just knew that she had always liked riding the bus, in elementary school at least.

Here comes the evasion, she thought to herself.

"I just need to get there early today to practice for

chair tests that are coming up."

That wasn't really a lie. I could totally get some extra practice in today before class. I'm sure Mr. Tremelo will be in his office early this morning and wouldn't mind if I sat in the band room until class started.

"Don't you practice enough at home, Demi? We barely see you anymore now that the school year has started."

"It's really important, Dad! I got ninth chair."

"Oh, alright then. Just don't overdo it. Remember to make time to have fun. Middle school was some of my favorite years when I was your age."

"I hear you. I'll try, Dad," Demi said, following him out to the car.

As the school day passed, Demi wrestled with the nagging undercurrent that hummed around her as she tried to figure out what had happened between her and Angelica to put them at odds with each other.

When the final school bell sounded, Demi's thoughts rooted her like a tree, not letting her move an inch, simply watching other students as they filed out of the square.

And soon, the bus with Angelica on board pulled off without its flute-toting passenger. Demi watched from behind the entrance doors as the bus disappeared down the street... becoming a yellow speck... then nothing at all as it turned down a narrow street toward its first stop.

I can't make a habit of this, Demi thought to herself, walking towards the band room. She was sure Mr. Tremelo would still be there, cleaning up his classroom and preparing the boards for the next day's lessons. And, sure enough, when she looked through the window into his room, there he was.

Mr. Tremelo had some light classical music playing through the speakers mounted on each corner of the band room's ceiling as he tidied up his desk. There was a little pep in his step as he and his fresh cup of coffee made their way around the classroom, laying out sheet music on the music stands for the next day.

Demi knocked on the door and Mr. Tremelo looked up from his cup, smiling when he saw Demi.   He answered the door.

"Why, if it isn't another one of my 1st period students! Hey there, Demi! After-school rehearsals don't begin until next Wednesday."

"It's not that, Mr. Tremelo. I, well... ahh, I missed my bus and I need a ride home."

Mr. Tremelo finished taking another sip from his cup and looked out, beyond Demi, into the distance. She thought that perhaps a musical passage emerging from the speakers had caught his attention.

Maybe it's where his ideas are stored, Demi thought, because hers were stored right around the same place; *right between looking up into the sky and looking straight ahead, somewhere in the middle of those two.*

The music teacher then looked at her a little strangely.

"Come on in. You don't seem like the type of student to be missing buses. Frankly, there's nothing I can do without a phone call to your parents. I already have to take Shane home once he's finished organizing the music storage closet."

Shane? Did Mr. Tremelo say Shane?

Demi looked over at the storage closet and noticed that it was open and the light was on, some sounds of rummaging going on behind the door. She couldn't see inside unless she went over to the door and looked in, which is something she didn't want to do.

Her heart was racing right now. All the thoughts of evading Angelica didn't seem so bad when it came to seeing Shane in the bully's place.

And then there he was. He walked out with a trash can full of old items that he had cleaned out of the closet. He didn't even notice Demi until he turned and saw her standing there.

"Mr. Tremelo, I got all of the old music thrown away and I've organized the—"

He smiled at her. It was that weird, awkward smile again that she adored so much.

"Oh, hey, Demi. I didn't know you were here."

And, after a brief sputtering of sentence fragments and a phone call to her mother who had just gotten home, Demi, Shane, and Mr. Tremelo were out of the building and on their way to the faculty parking lot, where only a smattering of cars remained, as many of the teachers had already left for the day.

Mr. Tremelo pointed to his very, paint-faded-from-the-sun Honda Element, switching his briefcase to his right hand so he could get his keys out of his pocket with his left.

"You'll have to excuse the mess. I wasn't expecting to have to take more than one student home today." Her teacher looked at her jokingly.

"I can't have either of you sitting in the front seat because the seatbelt is broken, so you'll both have to sit in the back. Just let me get these things out of the back seat and we'll be ready in no time."

Both Shane and Demi just stood there, trying their best not to look one another in the eyes. Demi could feel her heart pounding through her chest.

I'm actually going to sit next to him! I don't know what I'm going to do! I'm going to faint, that's what I'm going to do!

If this wasn't one of the most well-placed moments of fate Demi had ever seen. Here she was, out of the path of the raging Angelica and, instead, about to sit next to Shane, the object of her affection (*indirect, somewhat overactive affection that he had no idea about, of course, but affection nonetheless*).

We would breathe the same air, share the same space for a time, laugh at the same jokes. SHARE A MOMENT!

The idea of sharing a moment with Shane nearly put her to swooning into his arms and fanning herself. She didn't know why, didn't care really. She just felt *something* for Shane. By all definitions, Demi had **a crush**.

She had only had a crush on one other person and that was in elementary school. It was to the nerdy but trustworthy George Meekins. She would never forget his name or the situation his name came with. She regretted telling her best friend, who in turn told the entire 5th grade class about the secret crush. Thus, Demi could never look George in the eyes again.

Mr. Tremelo opened the door for Demi and she climbed in with her backpack and flute case in tow, sitting down, all the while doing her best to put her things down and get comfortable, even if it were only a few minute's drive.

"You can get in over here, Shane. Just watch the debris on the floor. Some of the cups that I've left back there aren't completely empty."

Demi looked down at her feet to see a myriad of used coffee containers and empty coffee cups: from Dunkin Donuts, Whataburger, Shipley's Donuts, Donna's Cafe, Dooby's Cafe, Starbucks, 7 Eleven, Caribou Coffee, and even some other places Demi had never heard of. Demi and Shane did their best to keep their feet from crushing the cups of old, half-emptied coffee.

Mr. Tremelo climbed into the driver's seat, making sure his students were buckled in. He turned the key in the ignition and smiled back at the two of them.

"Here we go, ladies and gentlemen!"

Demi had never seen the world from a teacher's point of view. But now, as she looked out of her band director's car window and saw the last of the cars disappear from sight as well as the school, a great number of thoughts passed through her mind.

What do teachers do after school, anyway? What

are their lives like? What types of food do they eat? Do they sleep on the same types of pillows and beds as normal people?

When Demi thought about it, she didn't really know anything about Mr. Tremelo, with the exception of his peculiar fashion sense and his cups of coffee, which seemed more of an obsession than a morning pick me up, looking down at her feet at the cups upon cups of coffee.

Does Mr. Tremelo have family? A wife and child back home that he goes home to everyday?

For a second, Demi had forgotten that Shane was even sitting next to her. She was so lost in thought. That's when she heard Shane's voice next to her.

"So, Demi. What made you miss the bus? I've never seen you after school before."

Quick thinking. That's what this had to be! There is no way I'm going to say I'm hiding from a bully.

"I forgot one of my books in my locker and, by the time I got it, the bus had already left. What about you?"

Change the subject, and fast, Demi thought,

watching as Shane stumbled cutely on his own explanation.

"I wanted to help out Mr. Tremelo with things in the band room and I've been practicing my Solo and Ensemble piece with him. He's been helping me with the trouble spots. Plus, the school is getting new band equipment. The storage room needed to be cleaned out before the shipment gets here. At least, that's what Mr. Tremelo told me."

Could he be anymore perfect? Demi couldn't handle being around Shane anymore: *the love of music, an awkwardly cute guy, and an all around nice person that helps out when he can.* This was turning out to be too much for Demi to take.

Then Mr. Tremelo stopped at a local gas station and changed the dynamics completely. He called over his shoulder.

"Sorry, you two, but if I don't get gas soon, I'm afraid all three of us will be walking home. You guys want anything from inside?"

Like coffee? Demi thought to herself. Mr. Tremelo was probably going to get himself a fresh cup before filling up.

"No, thank you, Mr. Tremelo." Demi bowed out of anything from the gas station.

"I'm fine, sir. Thanks," Shane then said. Mr. Tremelo nodded and climbed out of his car, leaving Demi completely and utterly alone with Shane in the backseat.

Why do I feel as if I am doing something wrong? How weird. Chill! Demi thought to herself, trying to maintain a good breathing pace, trying not to allow her own heart burst out of her chest.

What? I can't be alone with a boy I like right now? Demi, get a grip on yourself! I'm too young to be dealing with these kinds of things!

"It's nice that you're helping Mr. Tremelo."

"Yeah. He said, once the new instruments come in, I could help him unwrap them, store them in the closet, and even label them. I'm kind of excited to see what brand new instruments look like."

In a few more moments, Mr. Tremelo was back with his coffee in hand. He opened the gas cap and began pumping gas.

His head popped inside the driver's side window.

"Can you guys hand me those old cups, please? I'll go ahead and throw them away. There's a trash can right here."

Both Shane and Demi jumped at the chance to take the attention away from one another and reached down for the empty and half-empty cups at their feet. At one point, Shane accidentally bumped his knee into Demi's.

Demi nearly burst inside with joy. Still holding a few empty cups in her hands, she just looked down at her knobby left knee as it sat pressed against Shane's right knee.

She couldn't believe it.

It only lasted for 3.7 seconds and then Shane handed Mr. Tremelo the cups out the window, his knee apparently being needed, soon separated from Demi's, never returning to that position again.

Her mind swam, her heart stopped and then started again in a rhythm she could not fathom or write into music. The rest of the ride home was quiet yet Demi's mind was alive with a flurry of feelings.

Demi was by no means planning her wedding, but the crush she had on Shane seemed to swell and move to the forefront of her mind. When Mr. Tremelo asked which turn he should make to get her home quicker, she was jarred back to reality with an elbow nudge from Shane.

"Demi, Mr. Tremelo is asking you something."

"Huh, what? Oh, you can turn right here."

Mr. Tremelo made the turn while drinking from his fresh cup. His free index finger pointed at the house on the corner.

"Oh, I know where we are now. I had a friend that lived on this block and we always called that house on the corner haunted."

Demi looked at the house as they passed it on the way to hers, just a few houses away. The old house Mr. Tremelo was referring to was across from where she caught the bus everyday.

"Why did you call it haunted, Mr. Tremelo?" This question issued forth from Shane's mouth, which trembled a little bit at the possibility of hearing a ghost story.

Mr. Tremelo just smiled in response and took another sip of his coffee.

"I didn't know you lived here, Demi. This is my old stomping ground." Mr. Tremelo pulled his car up to the curb in front of Demi's house and her teacher put the car in park.

Once the car stopped, Demi attempted to glide out of the back seat with as much elegance as her flute case, backpack and lunch kit would allow, barely making it out of Mr. Tremelo's car without dropping at least one of them in the process.

"Thanks, Mr. Tremelo! Bye, Shane."

"Bye, Demi." Shane waved at her then shut the door once she was away from the car. Mr. Tremelo honked twice at Demi's mother, who was standing on the front porch steps, waving in return. Demi and her mother both watched as Mr. Tremelo drove away.

"So, what happened to you this afternoon? Your father told me you seemed melancholy this morning and you got him to take you to school. Next thing I know, I'm getting a call from Mr. Tremelo."

After a short pause, Demi said softly, all the while

keeping her eyes to the ground, "I missed the bus."

Demi's mom nodded her head at her teacher's car that had just turned off their street and disappeared down another.

"Who was that boy in the backseat with you? He's a cutie."

"Ugh. He's not **with** me, Mom. He just had to be dropped off, too. His name is Shane. He plays trumpet in band."

"Shane? As in little Shane from Harper?"

Demi was hesitant to make her way up the steps next to her mother, who seemed to be in a weird state of thought at the moment. Before now, Demi had never seen the expression that was growing on her mother's face. It was a look of wonderment mixed with dismissiveness.

When her mother noticed she was still standing on the steps, she ushered Demi in.

"Come on. I'm not going to bite your head off."

-7-

"What kept me sane was knowing that things would change, and it was a question of keeping myself together until they did."

- NINA SIMONE

That following Monday, Demi's mom had the day off from work and decided she would pick the kids up from school, with Demi being first. On the way to Harper Elementary to pick up DJ and Gayla, she wanted to have "the talk" with Demi.

Good, bad, indifferent, Demi wasn't expecting the long, drawn out conversation that detailed the ideals of love and marriage as well as first loves, which as she guessed, her mother was thinking that she was on the cusp of having.

"Boys and girls are different, Demi," her mother

had started, which led to a somewhat over-detailed analysis of the human anatomy and more than dozens of blushing moments for the middle-schooler. By the time they had to pick up her little brother at school, Demi was well versed in the ways of dating rituals and how a boy should treat a girl and vice-versa.

Demi had only one question.

"So, how will I know if someone likes me?"

Her mother pulled the car in behind the line of cars for pick-ups at the elementary school and put the car in park.

"Well, sweetie, that's the hard part. Most of the groundwork is laid out for you already in regards to going out with people. Some will just come out and tell you. Others will look at you a lot and find reasons to talk to you, even if it's just for a second or about nothing at all."

"Why does it have to be so difficult? Why can't they just say they like the other person?"

Her mother laughed. "I wish I had the answer for you, dear."

Soon, Gayla was waving to them and skipping over

to the car, her lunch kit swinging in her hand, her backpack looking two sizes too big for her small frame. Gayla's kindergarten teacher waved and Demi and her mother waved back, almost in unison. Then, not far from the curb, Demi saw her little brother DJ. He saw them almost immediately and began walking to the car. He smiled and waved to his little sister who was securing herself into her car seat as he got in on the other side.

"Hiyee!" Gayla squeaked.

"Hey, guys!" DJ returned, climbing into his own booster seat.

"Hi, my babies!"

"Hey," Demi waved into the backseat.

Their mother pulled off once the doors were closed and the kids were buckled in, weaving her way through the crossing areas and parking spots for parents along the circular pick-up/drop-off area.

"So, little man, how did your day go at school?"

"Great! We had hamburgers, french fries, and apple sauce for lunch today!" Both Demi and her mom laughed.

"Sounds like a great day."

"It was! Oh, and chocolate milk!" Her little brother DJ was always so emphatic about the little things. That's what made him such a cool little brother to have around.

A few minutes later, Demi's mother was pulling onto their street and passed the same house that Mr. Tremelo had called 'haunted' when he had dropped her off.

"Mom, who lives in that house right there?" Demi pointed at the house at the corner of their street.

"I dunno, honey. Since we've been here, I've never seen anyone go in or out of the house. There's no car parked in the driveway or out by the curb."

Demi wasn't Nancy Drew or Harriet the Spy, but she had a certain curiosity when it came to mysteries. Sure, she had watched a few mystery TV shows and fell into the story and excitement of unraveling the mystery, but, when it came to the scary house at the corner of her block, she was fine with not knowing anything about it at all.

Demi had never thought of the house on the corner of her street as haunted, at least not until Mr. Tremelo had said something. The grown-ups didn't talk about it at all whenever it came into conversation by other kids and Demi didn't make a point of bringing it up either. The idea of ghouls or ghosts sitting in a house down the street from her scared the heck out of her. She didn't even want to look at the house as she walked to her bus stop for school that following morning.

But, somehow, her eyes connected with a dirty window on the first floor a few times, looking for someone or some thing to be peeking back out at her from behind those yellowed, frilly once-white curtains. She never saw anyone or anything, though her mind conjured up quite a bit about what lay inside the house.

The kids in the neighborhood stayed away from it like it had been taken straight out of the pages of a Goosebumps novel. Even during Halloween, while the kids around the neighborhood were trick-or-treating, they made sure to stay away from the sunken porch, the falling roof, and the broken, staggered sidewalk that led up to the rickety house.

Since she had been living on the block, Demi too had never seen anyone go in or out of the house at 1225 Carson Street or, as the kids referred to it, "The House at the Corner of Carson Street".

Whatever grizzly events happened in there to leave it empty and haunted, I want no part of, Demi concluded, taking her eyes off the house and the windows and anything in the vicinity that could possibly bring chill bumps to her arms and legs in fear.

If it wasn't one thing, it was another, Demi decided, noting Angelica starting up once she got on the bus. And this time, Angelica didn't stop her ranting and harassing until the bus stopped at the school. Demi did her best to ignore the continuous ridicule for the next several days, yet it was getting harder and harder to cope with each time.

Why is Angelica being so obnoxious towards me? *Why is she being mean to me all of a sudden?*

Demi couldn't figure it out and didn't have time at the moment to wonder about it, because she was knee deep in projects, practicing, sectionals for the upcoming Holiday concert, and caring for Clyde.

In fact, that's exactly what Mr. Tremelo started with when Demi sat down for his 1st period class while periodically drinking coffee from his cup. He had gotten a new cup with a spill-proof lid. It was metallic and very neat looking and appeared as though it could be spy gear if he were a secret agent.

It could easily be a missile launcher or secret tracking device, a grappling weapon like Batman uses or a hand-held rocket.

Demi smiled at the thought of Mr. Tremelo being a secret agent.

"Students, although it's months away, I'm going to put this information out there. For those of you who have been selected for the spring recital, this is it. You may think that having months to prepare is a long time to practice, but when you factor in holidays, weekend trips with your family and friends, school functions and standardized tests, the time I'm giving you actually ends up being very short."

Her teacher handed out some papers.

"This is the tentative program schedule for the recital. While most recitals have a traditional line-up, I wanted to do something a little different."

Demi looked down at the paper that was passed to her by another student.

Our teacher wants to put us in pairs for a portion of the recital? That's whack!

The list was filled in all the way except for a small portion on the back of the sample program. There were two columns of empty spaces side by side indicating that students would be working in pairs. No spaces had been filled in yet.

After the series of mini heart attacks that the students pretended to go through while looking the sample program over, Mr. Tremelo quieted them down and tapped on the stack of papers that were left. The class stopped talking.

"I know how it is. You like working as a band and a few of you do not mind performing solo and that's fine. I'm not against that at all. In fact, that's how the recital is going to start. On the first page, there are no surprises."

Mr. Tremelo paused, leaning against the grand piano nearby. He looked at his class for a moment, while taking a drink from his spy cup.

"For some of you, playing an instrument may be something you enjoy doing for fun and your only goal is to march during a halftime show at the high school or college of your choice." Mr. Tremelo gave the students a moment to let this sink in.

"But given that you occupy a chair in this ensemble, many of you have proven that you are willing to put some time in. This arrangement will only enhance your level of musicianship. Let me tell you some things about the real world." He paused and looked around at each student.

"There are moments, moments when you can't escape the crowd, when you have to work with someone you've never worked with before. It could be a percussionist, an organist, perhaps a harpist. Whatever the case may be, you'll have to adapt. That's how it is in the music business. And the best way to prepare... is to begin."

The class shifted in their seats.

Their teacher continued.

"I was not prepared to play well with musicians I hadn't worked with before on a professional level when I first started out. I don't want that to ever be any of you. You need to think on your feet and strive to be better and, by preparing for our recital with someone in this room, one of your classmates, you're doing just that."

The rest of the day was a blur for Demi. She could see the dazed looks on a few of her band mates' faces as well. At the end of the day, Demi tried to figure out with whom she could see herself spending a lot of time with in order to have a decent performance.

Demi sat down in an empty seat near the back of the bus, Mr. Tremelo's words still echoing in her head.

'You need to think on your feet. Strive to be better,' Mr. Tremelo said, Demi thought to herself.

Demi's mind refused for some reason to grasp the concept of changing the dynamics of how she had been doing things. She had become comfortable with her approach over the last few years, as Mr. Wayne had taught her.

Demi had totally forgotten about Angelica until --

"WAKE UP!! What's your problem, flute geek?" Demi could feel Angelica's knees pressing into the back of her seat, almost making her drop her flute case and lunch kit.

"Would you stop, Angelica!" Demi's focus was broken now and she was a bit nervous. Angelica could sense this and continued anyway.

"What is it, Deeeee-meeee? Did I break your concentration? And no, I'm not going to stop! Why should I? It's a free country and I'm sitting in my own seat on the bus!"

"Don't you have something better to do?"

Angelica laughed at the thought. "Of course I don't! That's why I'm messing with you, Deeee-meeee! Because it's fun!"

Again, Angelica repeatedly kicked and pressed her knees into the back of Demi's seat, causing Demi to drop her backpack, flute case, band folder, and lunch kit on the floor in the process.

Demi turned around, smacking the back of her seat with her hand. It surprised Angelica and she flinched, falling back into her seat.

"Stop calling me that! That's not how you say my name and you know it! And you made me drop my stuff! Why are you staying on the bus past your stop again today?"

"I'm staying with my father today, not that it's any of your business," Angelica called back in return, continuing her attitude.

The bully in Angelica seemed to be waiting for this moment to happen. Demi was up and seemingly angry. Angelica had gotten what she wanted. And she struck back.

"You slapping that seat like that makes me think you wanna hit me. Go ahead! I didn't **make** you drop anything! You need to keep hold of your stuff better! Act like you want to swing at me again and you'll be sorry! I can promise you that! You mad? You want to do something about it?"

Those were the makings of a fight, Demi thought to herself. She knew what fighting words were and she never wanted to fall into that moment where she lost her cool, but she had just made a big mistake, letting her emotions get the upper hand. She allowed Angelica to get to her when she was least expecting it.

Demi didn't get a chance to answer. Just outside, she could see that the bus was approaching her stop. But Angelica kept eye contact and didn't want it to stop.

"Answer me! Do you want to make something of it?"

"No, Angelica."

"Cause you're scared? Is that why? You better be scared!"

"No, because I don't have a reason to fight you. And this is my stop."

"One day, you're not going to have an excuse." Angelica got up in Demi's face. By this time, the whole crowd of students on the bus were watching with rapt attention, their mouths open, eyeballs on all that was transpiring before them.

Demi grabbed up her backpack, band folder, and lunch kit and followed the other bus riders off the bus. The hydraulic doors closed behind her with a hiss.

The bus drove off, Angelica's scowl clearly defined

in one of the bus' windows. The plume of dust was vast as Demi walked in the direction of her house and then stopped. Each of the other students' footsteps had diminished until she was standing completely alone.

And without her flute case.

-8-

"If you learn from a loss you have not lost."

-AUSTIN O'MALLEY, Keystones of Thought

Wait! Wait! I left my flute on the bus, Demi screamed, but it was only in her mind. No one could hear her plea. The kids that had gotten off the bus with her were all walking towards their homes, but she just stood there, her right hand empty where the flute case should have been clenched tightly at her side. The bus had already turned onto another street.

How in the world am I going to get my flute back?

Demi felt the frustration and the helplessness well up inside her. She was mad at Angelica, at Mr. Tremelo for demanding so much from just a little, first-year middle schooler, and she was upset with herself for leaving her flute on the bus because she had gotten scared and panicked in the last few moments and let herself get so unfocused.

There, at the bus stop, following a deep sigh, she cried. She let it all out, allowing herself some time to think on what she was going to do next.

Should I go home and wait to tell mom what happened? It's PTA night at Harper and Mom and Dad won't be home for hours. Should I get on my bike and try finding the bus as it makes its route through the neighborhood? Does the bus even go back to the school after it's done?

Demi didn't believe so. She had heard that many of the bus drivers take their buses home with them or drop them off at a bus lot during the week. Whatever the theory, Demi's flute was long gone by now.

As the dust settled from the bus' departure, Demi realized that she wasn't alone.

She had consciously trained herself to keep her eyes away from 'The House on the Corner of Carson Street,' but her eyes met with another pair of eyes just outside the old house on the corner.

For a moment, Demi's heart stopped and her mouth went dry. As her heart slowly started to beat again, an old woman was standing out on the sidewalk, staring right back at Demi. She wore a light blue, long-sleeved housedress. Her hair was pulled straight back with a few locks tucked behind each of her ears.

She didn't seem to be a ghost or ghoul and certainly didn't look the part of groundskeeper, so Demi resolved within herself that this woman was the owner of the run-down home. The old woman didn't seem vicious or commanding at all. In fact, her smile was disarming to Demi and so was her voice. It was soft and calm, like a Billy Strayhorn ballad -- inspiring, yet a little sad at the same time.

"What's wrong, little one?"

It took a second for Demi to speak. "I just lost something."

"Oh no. What have you lost?"

"Something very important. It was my instrument."

The old lady's dark brown eyes flared with life.

"Instrument, you say?"

"Yes. My old band director gave it to me. I can't

believe I left it on the bus. I don't think my parents can buy me another one right now."

When Demi thought about losing her flute, tears came to her eyes and she began to cry again. The old lady waved her closer.

"Come here, dear."

For some reason, Demi didn't know why, she walked across the street and let the old woman hug her. It felt good to be comforted. Plus, the old woman was soft and gentle in the way she looked and in the tone of her voice.

"There's no need to be upset. What is your name, child?"

"Demi. Demi Woods."

The old woman was quiet for a time, letting Demi's sadness slowly sink away. Then she answered back. Demi could hear the answer vibrate through the old lady's limbs and in her chest.

"My name is Mrs. Aza." The old lady slowly backed away from Demi, smiling down at her. She was nearly a foot taller than Demi, *almost the same height as my grandma and she smelled like her too*, Demi thought to herself. *Honeysuckle.*

"I have some good news for you, darling."

Demi couldn't possibly know what this stranger would have to tell her that would make her feel better, but she was inclined to listen anyway.

"I happen to know Winston."

Demi had no idea what Mrs. Aza was talking about.

"Who is Winston?"

"Oh, I'm sorry, dear. You may know him by his last name, Mr. Buds; your bus driver."

Demi's eyes lit up when this finally sunk in.

"You know Mr. Buds?" Mrs. Aza nodded her head.

"I'm sure we can get your flute back."

"Really? How? I mean, thank you. But how?" Demi felt a great relief come over her and she hugged Mrs. Aza tightly, forgetting that they had just hugged moments before.

"Well, dear. I can give him a call for you. You're more than welcome to wait inside until Mr. Buds comes back by with your flute. I can make us some tea while we wait."

There was something about this kind, old lady that

made Demi think she could trust her and did not hesitate to follow her. The idea of actually going inside 'The House on the Corner of Carson Street' no longer scared her, but felt more like the first steps towards facing her fears about the house and getting her flute back.

Mrs. Aza led Demi up the sidewalk to the front porch of her home and opened the screen door, then the front door in a few quick movements of her arms.

Demi had never seen the inside of any of the houses in her new neighborhood besides her own and certainly not this one. Nor had she heard of anyone in her neighborhood being brave enough to even look in the windows of Mrs. Aza's house to get a peek. She followed the old woman through the foyer and into the kitchen.

"I don't have many visitors, so please excuse anything you may find to be out of place."

Mrs. Aza couldn't be more wrong. It was a beautiful place, a home like none Demi had ever seen. Besides it being completely immaculate and well organized, Mrs. Aza had played a part in a bigger spectrum of life than

Demi could ever know or imagine.

All over the walls in the foyer and the living room, which they passed through to get to the kitchen, there were framed pictures, plaques, and certificates from days gone by. And, in nearly every one of the pictures, Mrs. Aza was present, smiling a beautiful smile, standing next to some well-dressed person or persons.

"Wow, are you famous?"

Mrs. Aza giggled. "I had my time in the limelight at one point in time, but that's all over now. I prefer a simpler life, one that's not spinning so fast around me."

Demi nodded, thinking about the past few days of her life. "I think I understand what you mean."

As they made their way into the kitchen, Demi noticed that there were thriving plants hanging from pegs on the ceiling and some in planters on small ornate stools. They were all well manicured and vibrant in color.

The kitchen cabinets were made of white, textured wood grain and the floor tiles matched the wood. It was very rustic and antique looking. Demi really liked it a lot. In the center of the kitchen there were four chairs with back and seat cushions of a bright floral pattern and a matching tablecloth on the circular table. Motioning to the table and chairs, Mrs. Aza bade Demi to sit down.

"I'll go call Winston and put the water on for the tea." Mrs. Aza left and went into the living room for a moment shortly after putting the water on the stove to boil.

Water on for the tea, Demi thought to herself, familiar only with ice-cold sweet tea that her mother made on the regular during the warm, summer days, which, in Texas, was all the time.

Demi took her belongings and sat them in the seat next to her. She looked around at all of the plants and beautiful pots that held them.

Most of the pots had designs on them; slight marks and discolorations that made each of them different or unique. Some of them even had small shapes and pictures drawn on them; little animals, geometric patterns and waves were carved into their sides.

"Ah, I see you like my plants." The old woman soon

returned, smiling at Demi.

"They're very pretty. I love your flower pots."

"Thank you. I molded them and fired them myself some years ago. I have always loved plants and flowers but never had the time to tend to them in my youth. Instead of buying pots, I decided to begin making my own. You know, make them more personal."

"That's really creative. We have a pottery class at my school."

"Oh, that's nice. You'll find out for yourself how one can spend hours at a time on just one small detail and never realize it. I'm sure that's how music is for you though, right?"

Demi nodded her head.

"Don't you worry, dear. You'll soon have your flute back in your possession."

Demi's whole body relaxed and rejoiced in the moment.

"Thank you so much."

Demi and the old woman who resided in 'The House on the Corner of Carson Street' laughed and talked for what felt like hours.

Suddenly, there was a shrill whistling sound coming from Mrs. Aza's stove and Demi's eyes grew wide with fear. Mrs. Aza saw Demi's reaction and patted her on the shoulder lightly.

"Don't you worry, Demi. That's just the teakettle letting me know that the water's boiling. It'll only take a moment."

In a jiffy, Mrs. Aza returned with a tea tray filled with small finger food desserts and a warm kettle of tea and two teacups.

Demi was about to have a real-life, live tea party for the first time.

-9-

"Give your love, live your life each and every day. And keep your hand wide open. Let the sun shine through 'cause you can never lose a thing if it belongs to you."

-ABBEY LINCOLN

You can learn a lot from a person in just a few minutes, Demi took note, looking down at the Warm Vanilla Roast tea in front of her. The little dessert cakes on the colorful plate reminded her of Alice's Adventures in Wonderland and the Mad Hatter's Tea Party in the story.

"When you pour the warm water in, the whole place smells like warm vanilla."

Demi sniffed the air and could smell the hint of fragrant vanilla coming from the two cups in front of them.

"It smells delicious. Thank you," said Demi. She then stirred her cup of tea mixed with honey and cream with a small teaspoon that Mrs. Aza had given her.

The old woman breathed in the aroma that rose from her cup's contents before taking her first sip, her pursed lips savoring the flavor. She licked her lips lightly and set the cup back down on the tea tray.

"So, dear, tell me more about yourself. What is it you do? What are you interests?"

Demi took a quick sip of her tea. It was delicious and warm and it soothed all the doubts and fears that she had about this house and its resident.

She is a nice lady.

"I don't really watch television that much. Or movies for that matter."

"Well, that's a good habit to keep away from. It limits your mind from thinking on its own because it constantly force feeds you a false sense of reality and robs you of time you'll never get back."

"Wow... I never thought of it that way."

Mrs. Aza laughed and shrugged her shoulders. "I

don't really know. I've just seen some folks waste away in front of the television. You must take time to 'still' your mind. This is true for everyone. "

"What does 'still my mind' mean?"

"Well, dear, that is when you clear your mind of everything and just be still."

"I'll keep that in mind, Mrs. Aza."

"You do that, dear."

"I mostly play the flute. I haven't had time, or made time, to do much else."

"I also like taking walks with my dog. Before we moved to this neighborhood, every morning during the summer, Clyde and I would walk through Shamrock Park to an open field that felt like it went on forever. I would stand there with him and feel the sun on my face and, with my flute, I'd play whatever my heart desired. If I could remember what I had played, when I got home, I'd write it down and if I couldn't remember it, I would leave it there, back there, in that moment. Clyde has been sick recently though," she added in, taking one of the dessert cakes from the dainty plate.

"Oh, that's too bad about your dog. I know how

children get when they bond with an animal. I had a dog once, too. I was probably about your age. That was the kindest, nicest dog I ever did know."

"That's how Clyde is to me. He's my best friend."

"Clyde? What ever gave you the idea for that name?"

Demi smiled, the thoughts coming back to her like frenzied, energy-drink laden memories that wanted her to share all the details at once.

"His full name is Super Clyde the Wonder Dog- Clyde for short. Mom and Dad got him for me when I was little. I used to put a dishtowel around his neck under his leash and he would run around with me in the yard. And, when we'd go swimming, he'd always try to save everyone in the pool or at the beach. I guess he thought we were all drowning or something. The name just stuck after that."

The conversation continued until Mrs. Aza seemed to look right into Demi's aching heart and asked, "What in the world is troubling you, Chil'? I see you." Demi took a breath and turned her head away from the old woman as though she was embarrassed for not being able to hide her fear. Slowly she began, "There's this girl on my bus who is very mean to me. She frightens me."

In this moment, tears began to fall from Demi's eyes. "She is really pretty and popular. Because of her, a lot of the other kids on the bus pick on me, too. I thought she was my friend. Now, everyday, I do everything I can think of to dodge her in the hallways. I usually manage to go unnoticed by her during the school day, but on the bus, I can't escape her. Sunday nights are the worst for me because I know I'll have to endure being on the bus, again, everyday, from Monday until Friday." Demi wiped her tears away and continued.

"While trying to build up the courage to stand up to her today, I got distracted. That's how I ended up leaving my flute behind."

"Do you know how beautiful you are, Ms. Woods?"

Demi, startled, gave a small, "Thank you."

"That is not a compliment, Chil', that's a fact. We are all beautiful. You must begin, right this minute, to think highly of yourself. That girl must think highly of you or she wouldn't be so focused on you." Mrs. Aza paused a moment before she continued.

"Thank you for sharing that with me, Demi. This is not something you should have tried to keep to yourself. You have people around you who care. They will hardly be able to fight your battles throughout your life, but quite often they can steer you in the right direction, encourage you, and perhaps remind you or help reveal to you how special and powerful you are already. No fear. Now. Build yourself up today and everyday hereafter. And for goodness sakes, don't sit on the back of the bus! Who told you that you have to subject yourself to pain? Hurt people do exactly that! They hurt people."

Mrs. Aza took a drink from her cup and smiled.

"Happy, loving people want to see others happy. Sit on the front of the bus. Sit where you feel safe. And, the next time you graciously allow that devil to look you in the eye, tell her to leave you alone, but not with words. Words are very powerful, but so is silence. Speak with your eyes and communicate with your heart, to the very core of her, and she will hear you. I assure you. If you don't feed that foolishness, it'll die."

Demi felt like she took a breath for the first time in weeks as the last tear dried on her cheek.

"Yes ma'am. Thank you. Thank you very much, for everything." Just then, Demi could hear the hydraulics of the school bus as it was coming down the street.

"I think that's him, Demi."

Mrs. Aza motioned for Demi to grab her things and to work her way to the front door.

"Remember what we've talked about today. Be happy. Use your gift, joyfully. It was so good to be able to meet you."

"Yes. It was very nice to meet you, too, Mrs. Aza."

Just outside, Mr. Buds spotted Demi and stepped off the bus with her flute case.

From inside the window of the house, the old woman nodded her approval and watched as Demi ran to the bus.

"Thank you, Mr. Buds!"

"Not a problem, Demi. I heard the case sliding around in the back and figured you'd like to have it sooner rather than later."

Demi was surprised he knew her name. There were so many kids on the bus that she didn't expect Mr. Buds to know all of them, especially her.

"Thank you for keeping my flute safe. It means a lot to me."

The bus driver gave a nod and got back on his bus. He smiled and waved as he drove away, leaving a small dust trail in his wake.

Demi looked at the door of Mrs. Aza's house. That old, metal knocker sat silently on the wooden frame that once seemed mysterious. But not so much anymore.

If kids knocked on it, Demi thought, *they'd be offered a real-life tea party and a beautiful botanical display.*

-10-

"Sometimes it's to your advantage for people to think you're crazy."

- THELONIOUS MONK

The next day, Demi decided to take a seat at the front of the bus across from Mr. Buds. And it worked like a charm. No one spoke to her and she loved it. That afternoon, she was darting out of her last period class to the buses to reclaim her new seat.

Demi ran past Mr. Buds who was standing outside the square with a few other bus drivers. She was the first student to get on. Minutes later, other children came and, for a moment, Demi thought the busload was going to be light until a crowd of kids came. When Angelica got on, she stood and glared at Demi. Demi said nothing, but to her own surprise she jumped to her feet as though she had been waiting for this moment.

"You have something to say to me, Demeee?" She looked at every feature on Angelica's face as though she were studying them. Somehow, Demi blocked out everything and everyone else and focused only on the girl standing in front of her.

Who are you, Angelica? And why do you feel you have to bully me? Are you that insecure? Are you that unhappy? BORED? What do you do when no one else is around? Does it please you to make me or others feel badly? You obviously have very little to be joyful about and, if that is the case, I feel sorry for you.

Focusing on you is a waste of my time and I don't waste my time, EVER. I value my time and energy too much to waste it on thinking of you. How can someone so pretty act so ugly? Obviously, it's possible. What is beauty anyway?

Demi was almost amused by the conversation she was getting lost in within her mind. She wanted to laugh out loud but didn't. She continued to look Angelica in the face and allowed herself this moment. She was a happy person and she knew it. All at once, Angelica seemed smaller to her; smaller and weaker.

She stood there looking at Angelica and a peace came over her.

If not with appreciation and respect, do not talk to me, ever, again. Ever.

Just then, Mr. Buds climbed on board. He motioned to Angelica. "What are you standing there for, gal? Go have a seat! We're pulling off!" Angelica continued walking to the back of the bus. And Demi smiled and took her seat at the front.

Super Clyde's condition was about the same and, over time, all of Demi's family kept watch over him. Along with Demi, they all spent more time downstairs playing board games at the dinner table and watching movies. Everyone was paying a bit more attention to their beloved pet.

Neither Demi nor Shane said anything to one another after the ride in Mr. Tremelo's car. But, Demi did catch Shane looking at her one day as they left band rehearsal to go to their lockers. She could see him through the slits in the locker door as she opened it. Several times, Shane appeared as though he was going to say something and then, at the last minute, decided against it. He would shut his locker door and continue to his 2nd period class.

It was one month before the band students had to choose their partners and, together, select a piece of music to prepare. Halloween had come and gone and Thanksgiving was rapidly approaching. Demi and her mom put out all the festive decorations for Thanksgiving; real fruit surrounded the cornucopia in the middle of the dinner table and some tangles of leaves. There were artificial vines along the table runner, which reached from one end of the table to the next.

Demi had not spoken to Mrs. Aza since that fateful day. She didn't feel she needed to mention the near loss of her flute or the old woman to her family. In fact, she liked having something to keep to herself that no one else knew about. Mrs. Aza had a past and a history that separated her from the norm in Demi's mind. Having knowledge of Mrs. Aza was something Demi would treasure for the rest of her life.

It was on a blustery day in December when Demi realized that she had no idea who her partner would be. She sat on her windowsill and pondered a while. No one had come to mind and she hadn't really taken the time to look for anyone who would be a good fit for her. Mr. Tremelo had not said much about the pairings. He allowed the students to take some time to think about it on their own. But Demi had not thought about it at all.

I wonder if any of the other kids are considering me?

She couldn't imagine that Shane hadn't already thought about it. She was sure he'd already decided on whom he was going to work with *and* the piece they'd play.

Demi didn't know what to do or who to turn to. She didn't want to seem less than proactive to Mr. Tremelo, who she was finally accepting as her new band instructor. And she definitely didn't want to talk to another classmate. It would seem like she had taken little to no interest in the matter until the very last minute.

Which was completely true, Demi decided, looking around her room for an anchor as her 'island' drifted further and further into the abyss, with only her on it. Then she heard her mother call from downstairs.

"Demi, I'm going to pick up your sister from ballet. You want to go with me or stay here?"

Suddenly, Demi got an idea.

It had been nearly seven months since Demi had last entered Harper Elementary School and it looked completely different to her as she went in to pick up her little sister, Gayla. She had told her mother what she was going to do and her mother agreed to wait in the car with Gayla and wait for DJ to leave his soccer practice while Demi ventured off on her own.

It was weird for Demi to walk through the brown double doors she had known for so long only to realize it now felt foreign to her. She didn't fit in anymore. She felt taller and, with a quick downward glance at the tiles on the floor, confirmed it only further. She had once been able to fit both of her feet into one tile. That was no longer the case.

And those white and primary colored linoleum squares were definitely farther away now.

Nearby, two 1st or 2nd grade students stood talking outside the school office. They seemed so cute and small. Not that Demi was so much taller, but she had been walking around so many 7th and 8th graders that she was now accustomed to looking up at other students or at least straight on.

I don't fit in here, anymore. I don't fit in here and I don't fit in at my new school, she thought glumly to herself. *Where do I fit in?* There must be some place in the world where she fit in and she trusted that, one day, maybe after she was all grown up, she'd find it.

She walked through the empty halls. Here, there and everywhere were reports that students had written, projects with charts and graphs that they had done in their first few months of being there. She took a turn down the hall for the 1st-3rd graders, looking at the colorful art projects made with macaroni, marshmallows, and Popsicle sticks. There weren't things like this on the walls in middle school.

There, she thought, *the world of the imagination*

changed. No longer could the little kid come out in you; you were supposed to be growing up; saying adolescent things, thinking nearly adult thoughts, and contemplating what you wanted to do with the rest of your life.

At this rate, college walls and dorms will simply be painted bright white with nothing on them at all.

When Demi walked to the band room, she was not sure she would be able to find Mr. Wayne still there. However, when she pushed at the slightly opened door, she found him looking over his lesson activities for the next day of school on his Promethean board. She was relieved and very happy to see him.

He smiled brightly at her and stood from his stool. "Well, if it isn't the one and only Demi Woods!!"

I stand corrected. This is where I'll always fit in.

-11-

"If you're not doing what you love, you're wasting your time."

- BILLY JOEL

"Mr. Wayne, I have no idea what I'm going to do." For Demi, that was the easiest way to start, especially with Mr. Wayne. She had studied with him for the last four years of her life. Since 3rd grade, Demi had been playing in band and Mr. Wayne had been her favorite teacher at Harper. She didn't know whom else to turn to. Luckily for her, he had all the answers.

"What's up, Demi?"

"Duets," she moaned as she sagged forward in one of his chairs, looking for consolation.

"I am feeling stretched so thin and ready to give up. There is still so much I need to practice on my own. I have set a pace for myself and I don't seem to have the time to check in with someone for *duets.*"

"Wait a minute. Slow down, Demi. It sounds like you've got quite an ordeal going on in that brain of yours. But wasn't that always the case with you?"

"Huh?" Demi didn't understand.

Mr. Wayne laughed as he went on to clarify.

"Demi, ever since the day you picked up your flute, you've worked so hard. It's not like you to abandon anything. Giving up on something so dear to you should never be an option. You have a great opportunity to improve when you take on such a project. Choose someone. Anyone. And, go for it, girl!"

Mr. Wayne turned off his Promethean board and closed his school bag for the day. He could still see the lost look Demi had on her face.

"It's going to be okay. Whoever you pick will either compliment you or benefit from being partnered with such an exceptional musician. You are very headstrong. You'll both gain a lot from the experience." He smiled warmly.

"Thank you, Mr. Wayne. I really appreciate that."

"Sure. I can't imagine that you are having any

problems transitioning to middle school academically. Is there something else that's getting to you?"

Demi sat a while and told Mr. Wayne everything. From not getting a higher chair in band to liking Shane, facing the anxiety of getting on the bus everyday for the last couple of months, and of course she didn't forget Clyde. Mr. Wayne, his wife, and their son had made the acquaintance of Clyde at one of Demi's birthday parties some years back.

Mr. Wayne sat attentively, listening to everything Demi had to say until she was all emptied out.

"Well, you're going through a lot right now. Trust me, I hate to say this and it'll probably be something you've already heard from one of your parents, but it's just part of growing up."

Demi sighed heavily and sunk further into the chair. Her mother passed by the music room. She peaked inside and said hello to Mr. Wayne, urging Demi to take her time so she could meet with a few teachers. For this, Demi was thankful. Mr. Wayne was like an uncle to her and she needed his words of wisdom at this moment.

"Demi, you're in good hands with Mr. Tremelo. I've worked alongside him within the district for a long time now and he's a very good music teacher. He's a little rough around the edges and his caffeine consumption is startling, but he gets the job done. You'll learn a lot from this experience."

For some reason, Demi still didn't look convinced. Mr. Wayne stood up from where they were and walked over to his music cabinet.

"I have something I've been meaning to give to you. You still have that old flute that I gave you?"
Demi nodded. "That's what I'm using now. It hasn't given me any problems. I like it. I think the tarnish and the old beat up leather case gives it character."

"You're right about that. And it is one very special flute. Well, there was something I forgot to give you when I gave you that flute. Maybe it was just me and not thinking outside the box, but we teachers have a tendency to get blinded by things of this sort all the time."

"What sort?" Demi had no idea what he was talking about.

Mr. Wayne handed her an old wooden box. It was the same length as her flute case but looked as though it had been made by hand. There were rough marks on it and it had been smoothed down in some places but not in others.

"This is the box the flute came in. That flute wasn't part of the school stock. It was a donation given by someone in the community long before I began teaching here. When I updated all of the instruments and catalog of music scores, I ran across this box. And it had a note with it."

Mr. Wayne opened the box and took out the small, folded piece of paper. He read it.

"'To whomsoever finds this flute. Give it to someone whose hands are the most capable of spreading the joy of music.' This letter demanded that it be given to someone, Demi."

"And you gave it to me?"

"Yes, I gave it to you, of all students." Demi was astonished.

"Why?"

"Because you were self-motivated about playing

and seemed to possess the gift of direction and dedication, even at such a young age," he added.

"Not to mention that I came across that flute when I was looking for one to assign to you." He folded the sheet of paper and put it back in the box, closing the lid softly.

"You have the ability to overcome anything in this world, Demi. All you have to do is try until you decide to stop trying. Don't ever give up until you've made peace within yourself to do something else."

It helped to see Mr. Wayne again. By the time she left, Demi felt recharged. She left the music room with the wooden box and letter in her possession. Soon, her family was all in the car and on their way home.

Demi sat the wooden box on the dresser in her room and was about to open it and look at the letter again but decided to go downstairs for a snack.

When she walked past Clyde's resting spot in the dining room, she saw a couple of pallets nearby that DJ and Gayla had made since they had began watching

Clyde as a team.

His sad, puffy eyes stared up at her in pain; his head lay just off his bed and his feathery soft ears hung to the floor.

After seeing Clyde and feeling the encroaching sense of sadness, Demi decided, *I need to go to the island.*

Once there, *on her island,* Demi laid across her bed. She could feel the tears well up at the corners of her eyes as she looked at the world upside down, her head hanging off the bed. She had moved everything that was close to the bed up against the wall. The tears began to overflow. Her eyes let the frenzied captives escape from behind her eyelids, knowing that the tears would squelch the pain that lay like a festering sore in her heart.

Demi cried.

Not at the world around her as it spun on without her, but she cried for not knowing what she could possibly do for Clyde.

After hours of practicing after her shift with Super

Clyde that night, sleep eventually overtook her. Every ounce of her mind and body needed the rest.

*　　　　*　　　　*

Her dreamed started with a single image.

Demi stood outside her family's old house, watching her family prepare for a cookout.

I don't know what it is about this family, Demi laughed to herself. Texas hurricanes brought lots of strong wind this time of year, however, the darker it became the better it seemed.

We love it! The cloudy, dark skies are dreary to most, but not this family.

Demi could see her mom setting out a blanket and a basket in the front yard under their tallest tree. DJ was riding his bike and Gayla blew bubbles as Clyde happily chased each one as they floated away. Demi saw herself sitting not far from the blanket, wanting to write a melody inspired by the sound of the wind. She closed her eyes and then felt her fingers on her flute. The movements of her fingers now became second nature to her. She began to play what she heard.

The melody, like all the others before it, seemed to write itself, but this time, as she started to play, something was different. The wind changed. She felt the change all around her but kept her eyes closed and focused on Gayla giggling nearby, and then all was well with the world. She played on and the wind continued to grow and change. The air around her seemed wispy. Not one word could capture the feeling that was wafting over her. Then something very strange happened. Everything was still and, this time, Demi did not want to open her eyes, but did so anyway.

Like a fog, something was hindering her from seeing what was preparing itself before her. As impossible as one could imagine, the air continued to grow still.

I am not afraid, she proclaimed. Just then, her eyes could see. As if on cue, the fog lifted and presented to her a door -- an outside door with no hinges and no walls. It was a beautiful landscape. A field full of sunlight and wildflowers as far as the eye could see. She knew she was now very far from the sounds of Gayla's giggles.

Where am I? The wind was again changing, however, and it took form and she could hear herself practicing.

It was her own voice that answered in response.

You are entering the Realm of Sound.

Demi was suddenly fighting back fear.

Like waves of heat, Demi could see the wind in a wide spectrum of colors. The wind grew. She turned towards the door again and could see a crowd of people standing there as though they were waiting for her to open the door. She cried out.

"Am I supposed to open the door? It's already open!" She felt that there was a doorknob present, but still did not see one.

Now, I am afraid.

*   *   *

She startled herself awake when she pulled the comforter over her head. Nervously, she looked out from under the comforter to her bedroom.

What just happened? Was it real? Was it a dream?

It all felt so weird.

After a moment, Demi got up and paced the floor. At first glance, her flute appeared to be missing from its case and, at second glance, it was there... as it had been, all along.

Just breathe. It was just a dream.

*   *   *

The next day of school was a Friday. For the first time in a long time, she had finally slept completely through the night. She woke up too late to practice before breakfast and she felt badly for having slept through it.

When Demi walked into Mr. Tremelo's room that morning, she was determined to find someone to do the duet with.

I'm not leaving school today until I find a duo partner, even if it takes me all day long.

Don't overdo it, Demi, she chided herself. *You're not desperate. Well, maybe I am, but there's no need to look the part.*

The class was filling up and everyone was taking their seats. Just as Demi took her seat, Josh who, upon being noticed, waved to her with a guitar pick in his hand approached her.

"Hey, Demi." He said as he sat in the chair beside her.

Knowing he was always soft-spoken, she leaned in towards him.

"What's up, Josh?"

"You got a partner for the duet yet?"

"Not yet. I was actually—"

"Want to be my partner? I mean, I haven't picked anyone yet and the recital, it's—"

Demi nearly jumped out of her seat. But again, she reeled it in, a little bit, and calmed herself before answering.

"That would be awesome! Sure, I think we could work well together. We live right down the street from each other, too."

"Cool." Josh paused. "We do?"

"Yeah, Josh. We ride the same bus."

"Oh, yeah. Cool!"

"We live on the same street. Carson Street?"

"Oh. Yeah, I live on Carson Street, too."

"Well, when can we meet to start rehearsals?"

"Since you know where I live, you can come by tomorrow morning. My garage door will be open. I'd like to start running some jam sessions in there."

Demi nodded and smiled.

That wasn't so hard after all, Demi thought to herself.

- 12 -

"Without music to decorate it, time is just a bunch of boring production deadlines or dates by which bills must be paid."

-Frank Zappa

It was the weekend and Saturday was usually the day to sleep in, especially after such a demanding week. But Demi approached Josh's house, the sun not even high in the sky yet and, just as he said, his garage door was open and he was playing a few notes of the song she gave to him on the bus the day before. He played the same sixteen bars repeatedly, as though he were waiting for her to jump in.

There were album covers on the wall and, to Demi, felt like a breeding ground for greatness. She was terrified -- more nervous than she could ever recall being, especially for a simple rehearsal. Josh was twelve years old and a strong player. Both of his parents were musicians. His mother was a violinist and his father a jazz pianist. Josh spent each of the past three summers at jazz camps where his father taught classes and it showed in Josh's playing.

She walked in and took out her flute. They played what was on the page, however a few times they allowed themselves to improvise, venturing away from the written notes for quite a while.

Demi felt the air around her change, as it had done in her dream the other night. As the notes resonated through her flute, Josh's chords supported every nuance and breath she took. Demi's eyes were closed, but she knew the vibrant colors from her dream were all around them, forming shapes again. Josh did not seem to notice what was happening, but musically he followed her. Every note they played was a conversation that their young minds were too young to articulate.

I am so thankful right now for my family and for my

flute. Clyde is going to be okay and I am glad to have Josh to play with...

... Hmmm, that was random.

Once Demi stopped, she heard Josh's voice break past his usual, calm demeanor, scaring her in the process.

"Ahhhh! **Yeah**, Demi! That was **HOT**! We gotta take a break! All of a sudden, I'm starving!" Demi laughed and picked up her phone to check the time. She had arrived at 10:30am and it was now 11:47am. "Did you record that on your phone?"

"No." Demi couldn't believe how much time had gone by.

"Dag, Girl! That was CRAZY!

"Yeah, it was cool. .... How did you feel, Josh? Did you see anything?"

"I feel great!! Woo wee! And we're just getting started!" He picked up his copy of her composition and read the title: **The Realm of Sound: Clyde's Soliloquy.**

"What's a soliloquy, Demi?"

"A soliloquy is like a conversation with yourself. Like your own inner thoughts."

Josh looked confused. "You mean, like how my great Aunt Lily 'talks' to herself?"

"No, goofball!" Demi laughed. "More like the thoughts you have throughout the day within yourself. You don't think much about it because, to you, your thoughts sound like your own voice. When I first started playing the flute, I went to the library and I found a piece called Night Soliloquy by Kent Kennan. It was too advanced for me, but I asked my mom to order it anyway. I still have not had a chance to learn it, but I heard it at a concert last year and thought it was really pretty... and a little sad."

"This past summer, for the first time, I began to write a piece with different movements and, when Clyde got sick, I decided to dedicate one of the movements to him. I used to wonder what it must be like for him. He is the only dog in the house and, if there **is** a secret 'dog language', he didn't have another dog in our house to speak his thoughts to. I felt bad about that sometimes. For some reason, when he got sick, that was the first thing I thought about.... Josh, when we were playing you didn't feel anything?"

"Hecks yeah! This new amplifier is killin' it!" Josh went over to his amp and kissed it, wrapping his arms around it.

Demi laughed. "Yes, it is!"

In a month's time, Josh and Demi had practiced her composition along with other standard duets for flute and guitar nearly everyday. The presence of her duet partner further solved the problem of Angelica the Bully because Josh began to sit with Demi on the bus every morning and afternoon.

Angelica never attempted to bother Demi anymore. She made a foul face at Demi from time to time but Demi never heard a bad word issued from Angelica's mouth again.

The only thing that bothered Demi was that she saw less and less of Shane in the last couple of weeks. She wondered if Shane had noticed her hanging with Josh and had begun to stay away more and more until, finally, Demi didn't see much of Shane at all.

As the spring recital approached, all of the students were excited. For one, the recital was coming up and two, Spring Break would come shortly thereafter. Demi had trouble deciding which one she was more excited for.

Although she had a few weeks to go, Demi dreaded the idea of standing in front of so many classmates, parents, and teachers during the recital, but she knew it was something Mr. Wayne believed she could do and he promised he'd be in the audience.

This will only make me a stronger player. She decided that would be her mantra.

The spring recital was in one week now. At home, Demi's parents marked it on the family calendar in the kitchen by the refrigerator. When Demi got home that afternoon, she noticed that her Dad was the first one to take watch over Clyde. It had come to that now, someone watching over Clyde almost hourly. It was easy to do for the most part. Dad lifted Clyde up and sat him on the couch for most of the day so he could watch TV with each person that took his or her shift.

Her father had quite a collection of music and created a playlist of comforting music just for Clyde. As usual, the house was filled with her father's music, but these days the selections were even more soothing and mellow. Clyde responded most of all to the impressionistic sounds of Debussy.

Demi's after-school routine started with arriving home, picking up Gayla and DJ with her mom, doing homework and eating dinner, all before practicing. On weekends, she would take a snack down the street to Josh's garage since their practicing gave Josh a bit of an appetite. Going to Josh's house turned out to be a very good way to begin appreciating her new neighborhood. She loved the walk and longed for the day that Clyde could take the walk with her.

As always, Josh's garage door was open and he was jamming out to the music in his headphones.

From a distance, he looked like he was playing the shadow of a guitar. The black lines of his legs stretched across the empty driveway and the neck of his guitar was like a great hand reaching out into the street. Demi smiled.

He's one of the only people I know who doesn't care about what other people think about him, Demi thought to herself, waving hello to him once she came into view from the shadowy street behind her.

When Josh saw her, he slowed his strumming down, nodding to her once to acknowledge that he saw her. Then he continued.

Good ole Josh.

"Hey, Demi. Three more days. I came up with a new introduction for your song. Would you like to try it out?" He took his headphones off and wore them snuggly around his neck as he spoke.

"Yeah, sure. I just need to call my parents and tell them I made it here."

"Sure thing." Josh put the headphones back on his ears and jammed out for a few more minutes until Demi was ready.

Once Demi called her parents and put her flute together, Josh closed the garage door. Demi had never noticed it before but he had soundproofed the room by putting a thin layer of eggshell foam on the back of the garage door to catch the sound. When he noticed Demi looking, he nodded his head in the door's direction.

"Yeah, buddy! The neighbors were getting upset. My dad made me put the eggshell up to keep the neighbors at bay. It's from his studio downtown."

"Good idea."

"Thanks."

"So, let's try that intro." Both of them smiled.

Something strong overcame both of them when they played together. Demi felt the notes fly from the flute, whirl into the sky, transform into something greater. This magical transformation went on for the entire time as both of them played. Josh was still enthralled himself when Demi finished her part, moving over to the wall. This time Demi stepped forward and pushed the garage door button. The evening light of the moon overtook her just as Josh finished playing the last few notes.

"Demi, what was that?"

Startled by his question, Demi opened her eyes. "What was what, Josh?" But she knew what question he was asking.

"I... I think you know. The colors... the air.... Demi? For real! What was that place? Tell me, please! I know **you know**. And, I know it's **because of you** that I saw it. Don't try and deny it. Just tell me what it was."

"I don't exactly know yet, Josh." Demi let out a long, deep sigh. "I've been calling it the Realm of Sound. Please don't share this with anyone! Not yet."

Josh first appeared to be concerned then looked up at her and smiled.

He paused for a moment, reflecting on all that he had just seen and heard. He could tell that this meant a lot to Demi.

"You have my word. But know one thing, Demi- we're going to rock the house!!"

-13-

"I believe that if you'll just stand up and go, life will open up for you."

-Tina Turner

It officially felt like doomsday was approaching Demi. The world had suddenly found her weakness and had come crashing down on her all at once.

There was no use going on, Demi thought to herself, as she stood next to Mr. Tremelo behind the curtain of the auditorium stage. The wall of red velvet was the only thing that kept her from view of everyone in the entire school, including the dozens of parents in attendance as well.

The host and head of the art department, Mr.

Davenport, smiled widely and looked out through his thick glasses at the audience. He loosened the tie around his neck and cleared his throat before introducing the next performance.

"Next, we have Demetria Woods on flute playing the Telemann Sonata in F Major Movement One. She will be joined on stage by our electric guitarist, Josh Sampson. Together, they will be playing a piece Ms. Woods wrote herself, entitled, 'Entering the Realm of Sound'."

Demi stepped out onto the dark brown mahogany stage. Her black patent leather dress shoes broke the silence just after the applause had died down from the last student performers, 8th graders Jennifer McTeel and Susanna Morgan. They both stepped off the stage at the same time, one going offstage right while the other one went offstage left.

"Go on ahead, you'll do fine." Mr. Tremelo said. Demi heard him but didn't see his mouth moving. Just then, Demi saw Mr. Wayne at the opposite side of stage, just behind the curtain, a thumbs up to her. She nodded and put one foot in front of the other. And she remembered this time to breathe.

This will only make me a stronger player. In a faint whisper, Demi heard what sounded like Mrs. Aza's voice: *No Fear. Be happy and use your gift, joyfully.*

Demi recovered, watching carefully as she placed one squeaky patent leather foot in front of the other, the applause breaking the silence.

Tomorrow, at this time, it will be over.

I can do this. I have been preparing for this very moment. In two hours time, this whole thing will all be over.

She put the flute to her lips, positioned her arms, elbows away from her body, and looked out into the audience. And that's when she saw them -- her family. They exchanged smiles. Her eyes spoke to each of them, *I love you guys.*

With a quick breath, cueing Mr. Tremelo, Demi played the first four eighth notes. What felt like an eternity was done in less than two minutes.

Hold still. Wait. Smile and take a bow. DONE!!

The applause from the audience made her smile from the inside out. With a wave of acknowledgment towards her pianist, she took another bow. She did not notice her partner Josh joining her on stage but, together, they dashed into The Realm of Sound's introduction once he struck the first chord.

And that's when Demi began to change the world....

*   *   *

Marty sat for a long time looking at the old man, holding his breath like a child waiting for a present. "Then what happened?"

By this time, they had eaten their meals and the dishes had been taken away. The only thing that was on the table was their coffee cups, the coffee pot, and the tape recorder that lay between them.

That's when the tape recorder clicked, signaling that the tape was full. Marty moved quickly to change it.

"It wasn't just some kids on a stage simply playing at a recital anymore. Josh played the first few measures and together they took a breath just before the entrance of Demi's first note. She began to play and no one could take their eyes off of her.

Marty, I don't know if it was the flute, the notes, or Demi herself, but the lives of the people in that auditorium were never the same again after that night."

* * *

It was the most exciting six and a half minutes of her life, feeling the music drive each note forward, to the audience, to those backstage, and to those in the lobby. Demi sustained one final note and dropped her hands.

Now I can say, that was fun, Demi thought as she heard applause and cheers for her performance with Josh. They smiled at each other and took a bow standing just inside the red curtain. The flute rested in her hands as she and Josh stepped back, but not before noticing Mr. Wayne, who was now standing in the audience. Demi was happy to see him. Her parents also stood, clapping as the curtains closed.

"Yay, Babeee!" Demi heard her father say. Josh gave a thumbs-up and they both headed backstage to join the rest of the students who had already performed. Now all they had to do was sit and wait for the closing remarks by Mr. Tremelo and the night would be done.

I didn't fall over dead like I thought I would, Demi rewarded herself with a deep breath and a fresh application of strawberry lip-gloss. As she and Josh headed for their instrument cases, Mr. Tremelo stopped them both. He beckoned them with his eyes and they moved over to him quickly.

"The crowd. They want you to come out and take another bow."

The two of them could still hear the applause. Demi peaked around the curtain and heard her mother laugh, "Come out, Baby girl!"

"Yeah. Get on out there, Baby girl," Josh laughed as he and Demi walked back out. Together they bowed in unison. Thunderous applause roared all around them. Demi could feel the goose bumps travel all over her arms and legs.

"We need to celebrate, Demi! That was rockin!" Josh gave her a high-five on the way out of the school's auditorium, both of their families introducing themselves to one another.

Josh's father Thomas nodded in agreement with his son.

"I think we could go for a bite right now, what do you say Mr. and Mrs. Woods?" Jasper and Olivia looked over to Demi for approval this time. Her father smiled at her.

"It's up to you, sweetie. This is your night."

Demi nodded excitedly.

"I could go for some ice cream!"

What started as 'going for some ice cream' turned into a chocolate feast from start to finish. Demi's father had led them all to an all-night diner. They sat at a long table with nine seats; Demi, Gayla, DJ, Olivia, Jasper, Josh, Thomas, Josh's mother Clara, and Mr. Wayne.

Josh's parents were full of compliments all night, stating how Demi and Josh 'looked the part of two who should be in a professional concert hall.' Olivia and Jasper agreed wholeheartedly as they finished their own hot fudge sundaes.

A little over an hour went by and Mr. Wayne, along with both families, soon said goodnight. Josh and Demi gave each other a hug and took lots of happy pictures together before they left.

Now that's something for the scrapbook!

Just as they left the restaurant, Demi's mind wandered to Mrs. Aza.

Mrs. Aza would love to see me all dressed up! I could tell her about my performance and how much of a success it was!

"Mom, do you think we can go by "The House on the Corner of Carson Street" for a minute? I want to thank the lady who lives there. She's the one who helped me get my flute back."

Demi's mother just looked at her, strangely.

"Honey, I think the excitement of the recital has gotten to you. What happened to your flute? What house are you talking about?"

"The house that you told me about, the one that everyone says is haunted?"

Her mother nodded in acknowledgement of knowing the house and then looked at Demi's father, trying to see if he could figure their little girl out.

Her father was the first one to respond. "That house has been empty for years, Demi. No one ever goes into that house. Did you see somebody there? I hope you haven't been going 'exploring' with the rest of the neighborhood kids. You know that house is old and could fall apart underneath your feet if you're not careful."

"No, dad! Just stop over there on our way home. I'll show you."

As they approached the corner of Carson Street, she noticed that Mrs. Aza's house had no lights on inside.

That's not strange though, no one's ever seen lights on in that house, Demi concluded, asking her father to stop at the corner just for a second.

"Are you okay, Demi?" With a deep sigh, her father looked over at his wife. "I knew it. I think Demi's pushed herself too hard this time, dear."

"Go on by there and stop for a minute, since she insists."

Jasper stopped the car and let Demi get out onto the sidewalk, tapping along in her patent leather shoes up to the porch, testing the porch with one foot before placing all her weight on it.

I'd hate to get this dress and shoes all dirty before Mrs. Aza sees them, Demi thought to herself, moving over to the door quietly. She knocked on the door several times and waited for the old lady to answer.

No answer came from the inside the house.

Demi looked back and smiled at her parents and siblings as they waited in the car and knocked again, this time a little harder than before.

"Mrs. Aza!"

Again, no answer from the inside.

Demi needed to take it one step further. She moved away from the door to the window, doing her best to take a quick look through the raggedy curtains. And what she saw nearly made her fall over in shock.

Nothing.

There was nothing inside the home. No plaques, photos, or certificates on the wall, no plants or items in the foyer as they had been weeks earlier. Not even the little dining-room table in the kitchen where her and Mrs. Aza had sipped tea together.

Did she move without anyone knowing, maybe in the middle of the night?

Demi went back to the door and tried the handle to see if it had been left open. A thick layer of dust came off from the handle, showing that no one had touched the handle in some time.

"Demi, honey, I think it's time we leave now, don't you," her father's voice was heard over the car's engine.

Perhaps I was dreaming. The memory of the meeting did feel like that place between sleeping and waking, Demi thought to herself. And, in that instant, Demi dismissed her encounter with Mrs. Aza as another odd dream that she would have to file away and figure out some other time.

When Demi got home, she went straight to her room with her flute case after saying good night to everyone, Clyde included.

Before drifting off to sleep, the last of her and Josh's performance echoed in her head as it had done on the stage. Out, over and into the audience, her music flowed in such a way that it found that familiar place in each person's heart as it had with Demi over the last few weeks as she had composed it.

-14-

"I believe my music can make the blind see, the lame walk, the deaf and dumb hear and talk because it inspires and uplifts people."

- LITTLE RICHARD

"Demi, wake up dear!" No sooner had Demi opened her eyes did she see the bright lights over her bed flip on, her mother shaking her lightly on the shoulder. Demi lifted, half asleep, still trying to discern what was going on. She wasn't awake enough to decipher what was on her mother's mind, but she heard the urgency in her voice and it made her instantly alert.

Something must have happened in the middle of the night, Demi thought to herself. She sniffed the air around her, rubbing her eyes. She didn't smell smoke.

It wasn't a house fire. She was glad of that. Demi was just getting comfortable living in this house and her loathing of it had subsided from what it had been when they first moved in.

"What is it, Mom?" Demi said breathlessly.

"It's Clyde. Come quick!"

It was too easy for tears to well up in Demi's eyes at the thought of losing him. She had fought through challenges and survived -- the antagonizing bully, losing her flute, having to memorize the Telemann, and performing her first original composition, which she had written for Clyde. And, boy was she thankful to not have her mind on Shane all of the time anymore, although she still liked him very much. She was finally able to truly catch her breath and the little girl simply could not imagine not being able to tell Clyde about her day anymore. Who would she talk to if he were gone?

Demi sat up and let her legs fall off the side of the bed, slipping her feet into her slippers on the floor. She followed Mom downstairs to where Clyde had been sleeping ever since he became ill.

Much to Demi's surprise, the whole family was awake. What seemed at first like a simple moment in time for her and Mom had become a family affair. But, of course, Clyde was family. To say anything less of him would be a lie. Demi saw DJ's stare of disbelief first. He had been the one to suffer most when Clyde first became ill, having lost his after school playmate.

Demi moved closer to him and squeezed him to her side.

"It's going to be okay, DJ." Demi did her best to use a comforting voice when talking to him.

This would be with DJ for years. He would be scarred from seeing poor Clyde take his last few breaths.

DJ nuzzled up to his older sister, grabbing her tightly around the waist.

Apparently, Dad had been sitting up with Clyde when things changed, Demi thought, still hearing some light music playing in the background on dad's old record player.

The excitement in DJ's voice caught Demi off guard. "I know. Can you believe it? Super Clyde is going to be okay!"

Okay, Demi thought to herself. And that's when she looked down at the doggy bed and at their beloved pet. Clyde had been sleeping there for days without moving except getting up, with help, to go outside briefly and then back inside to get something from his doggy bowl that was placed near his bed.

However, in this moment, Super Clyde the Wonder Dog looked years younger. No longer did he look worn and aged from the ailment and subsequent medication he had been taking since his diagnosis. He looked 4-5 human years younger. Even the spunk that Clyde had shown as a pup seemed to come back in every step that he took now, every playful roll and whimper combination he gave as he thrilled the entire family with his miraculous recovery.

Demi was dumbfounded. Here, she was expecting to have to deal with an emotional upset and she comes down to the real, actual Super Clyde, defying age and death in one fell swoop. Indeed, his name matched him perfectly. But it wasn't until this moment that it truly fit him.

And that is when she heard what was playing in the background. Behind all the giggles and exclamations about Clyde and his "superness" at getting better from something that could have easily killed him, Demi heard something she never thought she'd hear.

Not in a million years.

It's a flute. Demi went still. She listened and there it was. She could hear the melody as it wove around her. *It was Clyde's song!*

But it was more than that. Demi heard an orchestra behind the flute, breaking in and following along with the notes that she had created months ago on her paper, on her 'island' all alone.

"How is this possible?" Demi suddenly felt like she was waking up from the strange dream she imagined earlier that evening. Her father answered her.

"It must have been the medication. It finally worked its way through his system. Isn't that right, Clyde?" And the dog answered with a loud, boisterous bark of happiness, nearly tackling Demi's father in the process.

Demi made her way over to the record player and

looked at the spinning vinyl on the player, grabbing the album cover up in her hands. She was almost scared to look at it.

There's no way that anyone knows that song but me! But she needed to confirm it.

"Dad, where did you find this album?"

"At an old record store, years ago when you were just a baby."

Demi turned the cover around and just stared at it for a long time, trying to convince herself that she wasn't dreaming.

The album cover read: ***The Irresistible Flute Melodies of Aza Thompson.***

And, on the cover just below the title, a younger Mrs. Aza stood in the middle of a concert stage wearing a long white gown, holding a flute in her hands.

What is... going... ON.... here?

And it was then that Demi realized that Clyde was better because of the music.

How would I prove it, with an old album cover?

In a daze, Demi walked back into the living room, joining her family, who were all smiles. Her brother and sister jumped up and down in excitement that Clyde was able to jump up and down as well.

Demi could see tears in her mother's eyes and her father just placed his hand over his mouth in astonishment. He was, for the first time in a long time, speechless with the situation before him. He just smiled and relished in the delight that Clyde was okay.

When would it be a good time to tell them about what I've discovered? What if they're not ready? What if I'm not ready?

Demi walked over to the window facing the end of her block. She realized she would be keeping all of this a secret, at least for now.

Where did it come from? And most of all, why her? She looked towards The House on the Corner of Carson Street and whispered, *"Mrs. Aza?"*

- EPILOGUE -

Old man Devin took a deep breath once he was finished, looking down at the two cups of coffee that had gone cold some time ago. He didn't mind, not in the least. Both the old man and the young man waved away the waitress whenever she came near, continuing on with the story of little Demi Woods and her flute.

The young college student was still writing down notes from the last few things that had been said when the old man spoke again.

Marty sat transfixed at the elderly gentleman in front of him, of the story, and of the words that he waited for to issue forth from the old man's mouth. Already, they had recorded through two tapes and Marty monitored the second side of the second tape now, waiting for it to fill and give the annoying click that all old recorders do when they're full.

He had half-filled his notepad and many of the patrons had gone and more had come in throughout the few hours that the interviewer spent with this old man.

But it was all worth it. Every-last-second, Marty thought to himself.

"For such a long time, I never knew what Demi was about. It wasn't until I got a little bit older that I realized what she and all those who are chosen to be artists are capable of. What she had shown me," he corrected himself, "what she and others like her had been able to show everyone who came across their paths throughout the world, with their abilities was, and is, a gift."

Old man Woods got up from his seat put a twenty-dollar bill on the table and prepared to leave.

The recorder clicked its annoying click and alerted Marty that the tape was full on both sides. The young man looked up at the old man in disbelief.

"Did you know it was going to do that? Wait, is our interview over?" Marty asked, perplexed.

"For now, but I'll be in touch, Marty. You can be sure of that."

"Did she share her abilities with you? Is that how you were able to know when the tape was full?"

The old man smiled and grabbed his coat and scarf. After slipping into his coat sleeves, he tossed his scarf over and around his neck. He then plopped his aged, worn hat onto his balding head.

He looked at the young man with a smile, "That, Marty, is a question for another time."

The End

About the Author

Flutist and educator, Delandria Mills is a native of Houston, Texas, where she began playing the flute at age seven. She graduated from Houston's High School for the Performing and Visual Arts, earned her Bachelor's in Applied Flute with All-Level Teacher Certification from Prairie View A & M University, and then went on to earn both a Master's in Classical Flute and a Graduate Performance Diploma in Jazz Studies from Peabody Conservatory of Music in Baltimore, Maryland where she now teaches in the Preparatory Department.

In addition to teaching duties at Peabody, she directs her annual Summer Camp, *Kingdom Flute*

Works, of which she is the Founder and CEO. The camp began as DemiFlute Camp in 2001.

She has won both national and international competitions and has seven recordings under her name. Along with The Realm of Sound juvenile fiction series, Delandria has begun a series of children's books for younger readers also titled Demi's Flute.

-www.delandriamills.com-

About the Author

Riley S. Brown has been working on his own publishing company, Wunderlannd Press Publishing, LLC, founded in 2012. After completing his fifth novel, Riley earned his second Master's Degree in 2013 for Creative Writing for the Entertainment Industry at Full Sail University. He is presently writing on The Chronicles of Ar Solon and The Wunderlannd Novel Series as well as many other new writing endeavors that are being released nationwide. He has completed 8 years of teaching in Baltimore City Public Schools and is now presently living in Murfreesboro, TN with his son Clover. Riley is working on his PhD. in Literature/Literacy Studies.

rileybrown90@hotmail.com

CPSIA information can be obtained at www.ICGtesting.com
Printed in the USA
BVOW06s1547160815

413496BV00004B/6/P